1979 - THE END OF THE BEGINNING

Leo Denlea

Prologue

Thursday, June 2, 1977, 6:00 PM, Clifford Jones had just finished his last final exam at the University of Southern California and was making his way across campus to his apartment. Excited and nervous at the same time, he knew this was the end of four years of partying student life and the beginning of his adult life. He walked up Trousdale Parkway from the School of Business to Jefferson Boulevard and turned left toward Hoover. He lit a Marlboro as he waited for the light to change at Hoover and Jefferson.

The last four years were racing through his head. Damn, it had been fun. Buying his first car almost three years ago opened up the whole LA scene to him. They say, "Only a nobody walks in LA." No more RTD bus rides on Figueroa to get to his shift as a teller at the Bank of America. His battered '67 Nova, "Mabel", got him to work on time, if not in style. Her six cylinder 194 cubic inch engine was a dog, and the "Nantucket Blue" paint job was faded to a dingy gray color. The dent on the left rear door made it hard to close, but she started almost every time. He had seen the ad in the Daily Trojan newspaper, and bought the car for $400 cash. More than once, the tools and tranny fluid he stored in the trunk kept him from being stranded on the side of the road. Cliff had learned a lot about car repair while keeping Mabel running. Mabel had taken him all over town, to the clubs on the Sunset strip and Chinatown and the beaches up and down the coast.

Clifford Jones was a couple of inches over six feet tall, slim build, straight dark brown hair that was a little on the shaggy side, but short enough to keep the bosses happy at the bank. His face was a bit long, but the girls would say he was attractive. He thought so too. He didn't mind being alone, but was never shy in a group situation, and would go out of his way to get a conversation going if things started to get awkward. He was wearing his signature outfit: white jeans, white shoes and a mostly-white terry tee shirt. He would wear his army surplus tanker's jacket this evening when it cooled down. Cliff was always conscious of his appearance, trying not to follow any fashion trends but making his own statement with clothing acquired at hospital thrift stores.

Working Mondays, Wednesdays and Fridays at the Bank of America barely paid enough to cover the bills. But they were going to give him a nice raise when he went full-time after graduation. Not like that first year in the dorms, broke, selling pot to make a little extra cash. He had simple rules to keep it on the down low: only deal with people you already know. You could bring a friend with you. You smoke some first, so everyone is on the level, then we do business.

It had gone well for a while, until that one night. Two guys at the door, strangers in Members Only jackets. "Hey Cliff, we hear you have pot for sale." It was dark at the door, but Cliff could tell he had never seen these guys before. Bad vibes, nervous, undercover cops? They didn't seem like students. He replied there was no pot here, and who the hell said so? When they wouldn't provide a name, he slammed the door. The pot business was closed and the pot was disappeared. After that he didn't dare keep a personal stash, in case they came back again.

Cliff Jones had met the Persians a couple of years back. A friend had asked if he wanted to meet with some wild and crazy guys who liked to play drinking games. Cliff was up for that. The ringleader was a guy called Cyrus, "Cy" for short, and party central was his apartment in Garrett Gardens down on Flower. Liar's dice was the game of choice, and you needed to stay sharp. You would land under the table if you took too many shots for losing. Cliff ended up hanging around there a lot, getting to know Cy and his sidekicks Gholam, known as "Goalie", and Kamran, called "Kammy" or just "Kam". What he liked about the guys, in addition to the booze, pot and loud music, was that they always kept it together, just like him. If they were drunk or stoned, no one got behind the wheel and risked getting arrested. They were willing to try just about anything, like Cliff, but there were certain no-go's, like no horse, speed or dust. They might party like rock stars, but they weren't going to die like rock stars. They had plenty of money, but didn't get into the coke thing like a lot of other rich students. Cliff was down with that because he didn't have money for coke. Anyway, all coke did for you was to make you want more coke.

Cliff crossed Jefferson, walked up the pedestrian mall to 32nd Street, turned right, then left on Shrine Place. When Cliff reached his apartment house on Shrine, he climbed to the second floor and walked back to his room. There was a note stuck in the door: "Party tonight". No need to wonder what that meant. Cliff went inside and placed his pack against the wall inside the door. Feeling like a little mellow time he turned the stereo on to KKGO-FM to catch Chuck Niles spinning some straight-up jazz. The stereo was college classic, all mismatched components, and speakers from a seconds store (you could hardly see the scratch). They sat on a sheet of particle board which rested on a couple of dairy cases. The LP's were stored in the dairy cases. Against the opposite wall was a plaid sofa, found at the curb on move-out day last year. A stop sign sitting on a cardboard box made the coffee table, furnished with an ash tray and matches. A small kitchen was tucked in front of the bath and bedroom. The fridge contained half of an El Rey's Garbage Burrito and a six-pack of Coors. Cliff put the burrito in the oven and turned it on low.

While the burrito warmed on low in the oven Cliff got a copy of yesterday's LA Times from his backpack. He had found it on a table in the Student Union. The Want Ads had lots of job openings, but they all required several years of experience doing whatever the job was. How do you get that experience? Are there any entry-level jobs out there? Cliff figured he was best off accepting his offer from the B of A. The teller job was pretty boring, but the bosses liked him, and there were always some interesting characters wandering in the front door, homeless drunks and visitors coming from the Convention Center across the street. And the local merchants were a piece of work, too. You would see them every day, get to know them, help them out and they would still steal you blind any chance they got. One of the best tellers had recently been fired for a large shortage in her cash drawer. She didn't steal it, of course, it had been a certain bastard of a merchant who caught her off guard and shorted a cash deposit.

After dinner, Cliff swapped the white shoes for his steel-toed walking boots, donned his tanker's jacket and slid the beers into his backpack. The University of Southern California was a wealthy school with a large and well-guarded campus, but this was still south central L.A. You better be prepared for anything. Cliff locked up his apartment and looped around from 30th Street to 28th , then headed down Fraternity Row. He was looking for parties to get free beer and chat up sorority girls, but it was quiet and he kept going. He crossed Figueroa and went into the 901 Club for a drink. He had a cold beer and played Asteroids on a game console for a while. Nothing was happening there either, so Cliff walked down Figueroa and wandered into the Julie's at 37th Street. On football weekends this place would be packed, so loud you couldn't hear the person next to you. Nothing was happening there either, except the smell of stale beer and disinfectant. The same nothing happening two blocks further down at Julie's Trojan Barrel, so Cliff swung around the corner to Flower, went in the front gate at Garrett Gardens, turned left and jogged up the flight of stairs.

The door at the top of the stairs was ajar and Bowie's *Heroes* was coming out at full blast. No one could have heard a door bell or knock, so Cliff pushed the door open a bit and stuck his head in.

"Clifford!" he heard a shout. Then, "Cliff the spliff, come on in!" Cy came over and pulled the door open. "How ya dooing man? Great to see you!"

Cliff stepped in and took in the scene. Goalie was flipping through a stack of LP's, looking for the next one to play. Kammy was sitting on the sofa in front of the coffee table, rolling a joint. Rock star and movie posters on the walls. Empties everywhere. "Good to see you, man", Cliff said. "Why you call me Cliff the spliff?"

"Ho man! You're so tall and skinny and always wearing those white clothes. You look like a giant doobie!", yelled Cy. "Come in, get a beer, smoke this joint with us, relax man!"

Cliff said, "I brought some more beers, but they're probably warm by now. Let's get them in the freezer."

Cliff walked into the kitchen, dirty dishes everywhere. He put his beers in the freezer and grabbed a cold one from the fridge. *Rock and Roll Band* by Boston was coming up on the stereo. He walked out of the kitchen as Kammy was firing up the joint. Kam passed it to Goalie, then to Cy, and Cy held it out to him. Cliff handed it back to Cy and said, "Remember, I told you I had to stop smoking this shit. It stays in your piss for thirty days, and they'll make me take piss tests to get a job."

"Clifford, this is crazy, man. You're the dude who used to sell us this shit. Then you stopped selling it. And now you won't even touch it. Are you trying to become a square?

"You remember when I stopped selling pot? Those undercover cops, pretending to be heads, knocking on my door? They knew my name, address and everything. Scared the shit out of me. And now, graduation next week, going out into the square world to make a living. You know the drill: cut the hair short, wear the monkey suit, dress for success, build the resume, do the interviews: where do you see yourself in five years, and all that bullshit. You guys are graduating, too, aren't you? Petroleum engineers, right? Going to drill for oil in Alaska or Mexico or somewhere; strike it rich."

Cy said, "No man, we are getting the Bachelors in Petroleum Engineering this year. Then we have two years left. Masters degrees in the oil business. Then we go home to run the country. We're the Princes of Persia! We're gonna take over our oil wells and refineries from you Americans and run them ourselves. We'll still sell you the oil – we're your friends, right? Still buy your jets, cars and trucks. We just need to make more jobs for our people. There's not a lot of people like us back home. Most of our people are farmers. They're dirty, hungry, live in mud huts, can't even count to ten or write their names. We need to give them good jobs, send their kids to school, build a middle class. In fifty years we'll be as rich as you Americans. That's why Shah sent us all here, to learn how to run a modern country. That's his plan."

Cliff replied, "That all sounds pretty good. But why does your Shah have those stories going around about Savak, the secret police, beating up people and throwing them in dungeons?"

Cy went on, "Oh, Shah is all right. You don't know what it is like in Iran. You have no threats. Your neighbors are Mexico and Canada. Canada a threat, hah! We have to protect ourselves. We've got fucking Russia on our back. They want to conquer us. Their agents are everywhere, and they are turning our students into a bunch of commies. Most of us here at SC are okay, but the Persians over at UCLA are a bunch of fucking commies. And the rest are crazy fundamentalists like the Saudis. They want to go back six hundred years, put the women in black sheets, have religious police, no booze, no music, no fun, and everybody poor but the priests. We have to fight back, or those assholes will take over. We do what we gotta do."

"Anyway, enough of this BS. It's time to play Liar's Dice. You bring money, Cliff, so you can lose it to me?"

"Oh, I'm gonna to take your money tonight", bragged Cliff. "Now let's get those beers out of the freezer and warm up the dice!"

They played dice for several hours, drinking beer and losers taking shots of Jack Daniels. The game was tight for a while, but eventually Cliff noticed Kammy was looking a little out of it, too many shots, not even checking his dice. After calling "Liar" on Kammy three games in a row, they decided to call mercy, give him his money back and end the game.

Cliff asked Cy, "What are you guys doing this summer? Where will you go?"

Cy said, "Oh, the usual. We go home for a few weeks, hang out with the family. Then we go to France: Paris, Cote d 'Azur. Then London and New York for shopping before we come back here for school."

Then he asked, "So what are you gonna do this summer, man? Where you gonna live, where you gonna work?"

Cliff answered, "You know, I'm probably gonna stay at the bank. I don't have any other offers and they're offering a nice raise if I go full time. And I might as well keep that apartment on Shrine, cause it's cheap and close to work. So I'll be around here for a while."

Cy said, "You'll probably be a total square by next semester. But, if you're still partying then, come down and hang out with us. We'll still be here, the crazy Princes of Persia!"

One

Thursday, June 9, 1977, Cliff Jones graduated from USC with a Bachelors degree in business. Afterwards, he did keep his Shrine Place apartment and did accept the job offer at the Bank of America on Figueroa. After a few weeks of training at the branch, he was named Assistant Director of Operations. They had been trying to find an assistant for his boss Shelly, the Director of Ops, for over a year. Now that Cliff had his degree and was working full time, he fell right into the job. Six months later Chuck, the Branch Manager, took him aside after closing.

"You remember back when we hired you, we trained you here in the branch. We didn't want to send you downtown. We were afraid they'd steal you when they found out how good you are with numbers. But we can't hold up your career forever, so we are sending you downtown to headquarters for Operations and Loan Officer training. Maybe we'll get you back, maybe not. Shelly is kind of bummed, but that's not your problem. Whatever happens, we wish you luck."

Cliff was surprised. "Wow! I'm not sure what to say. I guess, thank you."

When the training class was complete, Cliff was offered a job as a Loan Officer trainee at the B of A branch on Wilshire and Mariposa. He jumped at the offer. After a few weeks of looking, he was able to find an apartment at 749 Alandele Avenue, just three and a half miles west on Wilshire, right across from the museum and La Brea tar pits. He could take a short commute on the #20 bus if Mabel acted up on him.

This was a big improvement for Cliff. Downtown by the University was dead quiet all summer, and when fall semester began, it felt weird to be a working guy surrounded by all those students. Up in the Fairfax district, there was lots more going on for him. He still went downtown every now and then to go to a football game or to party with Cy and the guys. But he was meeting people and doing things along Wilshire.

For the first few weekends, Cliff used the Pennysaver to locate yard sales and flea markets so he could furnish the new apartment. A new-to-him sofa, armchair and coffee table filled the living room. The old milk crates and particle board still served as the entertainment center. A round table and four chairs comprised the dining room, and a handful of framed posters sort of covered the walls.

Saturdays, he walked to the Farmer's Market for breakfast and light shopping. He played in pick-up basketball games at Pan-Pacific Park on Beverly, conveniently two blocks from his favorite new hang-out, El Coyote Bar and Mexican Restaurant. And Tom Bergin's Irish pub was just a few blocks away: a great place to watch Dodger games.

At the bank, Sally Brindell, the New Accounts manager took him under her wing and showed him the ropes. She was married and in her thirties, but still nicely put together and Cliff enjoyed flirting with her. Safe, probably. They had the same lunch break, so they ended up eating together most days. She let him know who was cool, and who to watch out for, both customers and other employees. Chris Noble, the branch manager, was cool. He pretty much left Cliff to do his thing, but always seemed glad to answer even trivial questions.

Some months later, he met Bridgette. Or literally, ran into Bridgette. He was shopping on a Saturday morning at the Farmers Market and pushed his cart around the corner. Into hers.

"Watch out there, clumsy!", she yelled. Tall, slim, curvy, ...a real fox! And she had this little grin on her face. She was amused, not angry. Cliff felt his ears turn red. Hold it together, man. Be cool!

He had started off on the wrong foot, but he really wanted to get to know this girl.

"Oh sorry", he said to her, "How did you know my name?"

She stared at him with a puzzled look.

"Clumsy?...'cuz I am?" She laughed. Good sign! He asked, "Is your cart in pain? Can I make it up to you? Lunch at Du-Pars?"

She smiled and said, "Clumsy, huh? OK, I'll bite, especially for a free lunch. Does that pick-up line usually work for you?" "This is the first time I've tried it. But I've got high hopes!" he said.

Two

It was January 2, 1979 and Clifford Jones was at his desk in the Bank of America on Wilshire. He was a little hung over and more than a little tired after attending the Rose Bowl the day before with some college buds. After a controversial touchdown that left the Michigan fans steaming, USC had defeated Big Blue 17-10. The celebration after-party roared for hours in the Rose Bowl parking lot. Cliff wasn't home til midnight. Sally and the others were giving him a hard time about it. He was trying to tough it out until closing time when his phone rang around 4:30 PM.

"Cliff, it's Cy. We're in trouble. We need your help man. We got to get out of here. Can you pick us up?"

"OK man, I get off at 5. Where are you guys? What's going on?"

"Cliff, you haven't heard the news? The bastards attacked my auntie's house! They burned my car! They tried to break in and burn down the house! We need to get out of here in case they come back."

"OK man, Cy, calm down. Did anyone get hurt? Where are you?"

"It's OK now. The cops chased them off. And some of them are guarding the house now. But the security guys took away my Auntie and the queen mum in their cars. So there's no one to get us out of here. We're up at the house on Calle Vista in Beverly Hills. Can you come get us?"

"Okay, okay. I'll be there as soon as I can."

Cliff was really puzzled. Did he hear "queen"? He looked up the address in his Thomas Guide and saw it was above Sunset and Doheny. Way up the hill. On the way, he put KNX News on the radio and began to hear bits and pieces about a riot in Beverly Hills. Persian students protesting against the queen. He drove west on Wilshire, went by his place and turned right on San Vincente. He took San Vincente to the merge with Sunset and stayed right to end up on Doheny, which took him straight to Calle Vista. When he arrived at Calle Vista, there were a lot of cops and plainclothes standing around, staring at him. Mabel didn't fit in this neighborhood. The only ones with a car like this up here would be the help.

A cop waved him over to the gates, which he could see were smashed. He showed his ID and said he was there for Cyrus. After a quick call on the radio, he was waved up. You couldn't see the house from the street. As he went up and up the driveway he realized it wasn't a house, it was a mansion. No, not a mansion, a palace! He parked next to a couple of squad cars and got out. He saw a worried-looking Cy come out a side door and walk over. Cliff was in a complete blur, absolutely clueless to what was happening there. He said, "Lucy, you got some 'splaining to do!"

Cy relaxed a little, smiled, remembering watching "I Love Lucy" while partying with Cliff. "Typical Cliff, nothing bothers you. Cool as a cucumber. You're still driving this piece of shit Chevy No-go?"

Cy looked thoughtful for a minute. "Actually...that might be a good thing, " he said.

Cliff replied "Be careful what you say about Mabel. You could hurt her feelings. So, what's the deal here? What are you even doing up here?"

Cy finally explained things. "This is my Auntie Shams' house. She's lived here for a while. She is Shah's big sister, the Princess. Her mum came to visit, that's the queen mum to you, so Auntie had all of us over for a new years movie party and sleepover. See, she loves the movies and she's got a big theater in there. So today we're having brunch, getting ready to leave, when these people start coming up the hill. They're in the street, breaking down the gates, coming up the hill from behind, throwing rocks, breaking windows, starting fires. We've got security and some Beverly Hills cops here, but it was too much for them. They called in the sheriffs and the sheriffs started tear-gassing the attackers. Fucking Iranian Students Association. Cops drove them back down the hill. Me and Kammie and Goalie were in the back, in the men's house. My car is parked on the street and I could see them starting to mess with it. I opened the window and fired a few shots over their heads, but it was too late and my car was on fire. Fuck those commie bastards!"

Cliff was dumbfounded. "So if your auntie is the Shah's sister, and she is your aunt, then who the fuck are you?"

Cy laughed at the Who joke. "Like I always said: We are the fuckin' Princes of Persia, my cousins Goalie and Kam and me. You just weren't paying attention Cliff."

Cliff said, "Dude, a lot to process."

"Yeah, I suppose. Anyway, let's get out of here. They knew auntie and queen were here, but they didn't know we were here. The security took auntie and queen away as soon as it was clear. They won't notice us, especially in your car. Take us back to campus, they won't mess with us there."

Cy, Kam and Goalie piled into Mabel and Cliff drove off. The guys were hunkering down in their seats, collars up to mask their faces. The cops were still below on Doheny and it was already dark, so they were able to slip out of Beverly Hills without being noticed. Cliff went east on Doheny, then turned down San Vincente, remembering when this was his safe route home after wild shows at the Whiskey. (Except for that one night when he picked up that crazy chick. Or did she pick him up? It didn't matter. No going home. That night was like a live sex manual, the Kama Sutra or something. He learned tricks and positions that he didn't even know existed. Then, she was gone and never seen again.) There were no cops that night on San Vincente, running down to the tee intersection at Venice.

Once he reached Venice Boulevard and headed east toward Figueroa the guys finally relaxed and filled him in on the details. "Shah is in trouble and he is not feeling well either. We think he is pretty sick, cancer or something. Here's the problem. These commies get money from Russia. They call big meetings and they give the kids food and hashish. Once the kids are good and fucked up, they send them into the streets to riot. Like 30,000 people at a time. It's huge. Too big for the police to handle. They are breaking glass, starting fires, looting, yelling and screaming. What is Shah supposed to do? Businesses are burning. Homes are burning. So he calls in the army to protect everyone else. The rioters attack the soldiers, throwing rocks, bricks, Molotov cocktails. What do the soldiers do? Shoot back. Now rioters die and they call Shah a criminal for shooting rioters. So now the priests tell everyone that Shah is a criminal and must go away. Especially that Khoumaini guy in Paris. Inciting riots and now he has convinced workers to go on strike. They're too dumb to understand: strike means no work, no pay, no fuel, no food. So if they keep striking they will be starving. And no oil going out means no money coming in, so government goes broke too. Then they seduce these student that are here in the U.S. and get them to demonstrate against Shah. They are so stupid. They couldn't be here in the U.S. without Shah paying for them."

"Today was different. We know they are always watching us, but this is the first time they go after the family. So they want Shah to leave, they want the government to collapse, they want all the ethnics to rebel. It becomes total chaos, then some commie guy will get on the radio, say he's in charge but needs help. Fucking Russian army will march on Tehran, just to help out."

The guys go on and on. It is good to let it out. They are calming down now, more pissed off than scared. Burgers and beer at

Julie's hit the spot. "I gotta get home – work tomorrow and I was pretty fried last night" said Cliff. "I'll check on you guys in a few days. Prince, you're going to need a new car. Something more low-key than your burnt Beemer. I hear there is a '65 Oldsmobile wagon for sale somewhere near campus. It could be big brother to Mabel."

"Fuck you, Cliff", said Cy, but he was laughing.

Three

During his lunch break Thursday, Cliff saw the front page of the LA Times. It had a photo from the Iranian Students convention in Northridge. There's a bunch of guys with bandages on their heads from the riot in Beverly Hills, and they have a flag on the wall with the hammer and sickle on it.

Cliff rang down to Cy's apartment and he picked up. "Hey Cy, its Cliff. Did you see the front page of the Times this morning? You were right about that Iranian Students group being a front for the commies. They hung a hammer and sickle flag in front of their convention. Right here in LA. And a bunch of the guys have bandages on their heads from the riot at your aunt's house."

"I told you so", said Cy.

Four

In the next weeks, Cliff Jones began to pay a little more attention to the news. On January 16th, the Shah flew his own plane to Egypt, but then flew on to Morocco on the 22nd. Then that Khoumaini guy showed up in Iran at the end of the month. By the middle of February he was asking Morocco to extradite the Shah.

Cliff was invited to a party at Garrett Gardens on Friday, March 23. "Just come down after work", Cy told him. Cliff showed up that evening and was amazed. The apartment was spotless, and there was a large round table in the middle of the living room. The guys were all neatly dressed, too. Cliff was glad he still had his suit and tie on from work.

"What's the occasion, guys?" he asked.

"This is Nowruz, our Persian New Year. Check out the table: we call it the haft-sin table and we cover it with seven symbols for a good new year. So, we have apples for beauty, garlic for health, vinegar for patience, hyacinth for spring, sweet pudding for fertility, sprouts for rebirth and coins for wealth. We leave these out for thirteen days to celebrate."

"Normally, we would gather with our family to celebrate, but this year is pretty messed up. Our auntie and queen mum are still pretty shook up, and they are basically hiding out in the desert. But Cliff, you are like family to us, so let's party!"

Cliff said, "Well, since you guys are dressed up like a bunch of waiters, why don't we hit the town. Prince, did you get a new Beemer yet, or are we going to town in Mabel?"

"Still working on that problem dude, but since its already dark, no one will see us in your beater."

"I'll tell Mabel you said that", said Cliff.

First stop, the Top of the Five. Cliff went up the Harbor freeway to 4th Street. Since they rolled up the sidewalks at six in downtown Los Angeles, street parking was easy. They got a table by the windows in the revolving lounge, and ordered rounds of tropical drinks and some snacks. They put an ashtray on the window sill and watched it move away. If your drink wasn't finished by the time the ashtray came back around, you had to take a shot.

"Hey guys", said Cliff after a while, "We need to get this party on the road. Next stop: Chinatown!" Cliff cut over to Broadway from 4th Street, and turned left. A car across the street had done a U-turn when they left the hotel, and it turned north on Broadway behind him. Odd, he thought, but the car dropped from sight and he forgot it. They parked on Broadway and crossed at Gin Ling Way to get to Madame Wong's. "Hey Cliff, isn't this the punk rock club you always go to?" Cliff nodded his head to the right to indicate the Hong Kong Low and said, "Close by, but no punk rock tonight. Madame Wong's has a Polynesian revue on the weekends. Hula girls, grass skirts, coconuts, hubba hubba! And the drinks are bigger than the Hong Kong."

So the guys got a table up front of the stage and enjoyed the dancing girls, Tanqueray and tonics and the Chinese snacks called Pu-Pu's. They gave generous tips to the most energetic dancers. Soon, they were chatting up the dancing girls between sets. At the end of the evening, the Madame herself chased the guys out of the place. "You stay away from my girls!", she shouted at them as they jogged laughing down the stairs to the plaza.

"Now it's time for punk rock. And some food before driving home", said Cliff. He drove the guys a few blocks down Broadway to 1st Street, then east to Alameda. Again, easy parking near the Atomic Cafe, over by the train tracks. They ordered big bowls of udon while feeding coins into the punk rock jukebox. The waitresses were all cute Japanese girls wearing skin-tight black jump suits. Nice to look at, but the cook in the back with the big cleaver knife made it clear that they were off limits. "Damn!"

By the time Cliff finished driving down deserted Broadway back to the Garrett Gardens, he was pretty clear and ready to drive home. He told the guys that he would be waiting in a gas line the next morning to fill up Mabel. Cliff drove up San Vincente to get home with no problem. He thought he saw that car from downtown a block behind him at one point, but figured his mind was playing tricks.

Five

Saturday morning, April 7th, Cliff Jones heard on the basketball courts that Lou Reed's tour would be at the Roxy Theater the first weekend of May. His basketball friend had music biz connections and Cliff was able to score two VIP seats for Friday the 4th. Cliff had gone on several dates with his friend Bridgette, but she worked full time as a paralegal and was studying for her J.D. at the same time. She usually said she was too busy to go out. Cliff did know that she was really into the glam rock, glitter rock scene, including Bowie and the Velvet Underground, so this show would hopefully entice her to go out with him.

He called her the next Saturday. "Hey Bridgette, it's Jones. How ya doing?"

"Nice to hear from you Jones. I'm just like always, up to my ears in work. How are you doing?

"Oh, just the usual at the B of A. Giving away their money as fast as I can. But hey, I called to ask you out. I know you're always busy, but I've got two tickets for the Lou Reed show at the Roxy on May 4. It's a Friday, so maybe you can take a night off? What do you say?"

"Lou Reed? Thee Lou Reed? Andy Warhol, Velvet Underground and all that Lou Reed?

"Yes, the very one!

"Wow! For sure, I am there! What do you want me to do?"

"I can pick you up at your place, around 8. Friday, May 4. Your place on Arnaz, by 3rd?"

"That's it. I'll be waiting! See you then Jones." (Fist pump!)

Six

On May 4, Cliff Jones was figiting at his desk at the Bank of America. The clock seemed to be running slowly, and business was really slow for a Friday. Fridays were paydays, usually the busiest day of the week. Everyone was talking about it. His boss, Chris, the branch manager was theorizing that everyone was trying to fill up their cars, since odd-even gas days was starting on Monday. Cliff couldn't get out of there fast enough. He barely paid attention to the car parked across Wilshire with two guys in the front seat. He thought he had seen that car in the exact spot two or three times in the last month.

Cliff found a gas line and joined it. This was becoming a regular occurrence with all the panic over the gasoline supply. Once Cliff got his tank topped off, he headed home. Mabel's 194 cubic inches and in-line six cylinders only generated 120 horse power, so she was no muscle car. But her good gas mileage and 16 gallon gas tank meant he would do better than most when those odd-even gas lines got going next week. And he could take the RTD number 20 bus if gas really became scarce.

At home, Cliff put Lou Reed's *Rock N Roll Animal* on the turntable. He shaved (again) and showered, then dressed in his usual white terry tee shirt, white jeans, steel-toed walking boots and tanker jacket. About a quarter to eight, he drove west on 8th Street, then north on San Vincente until it merged with Burton. A left on Arnaz, and he was there. Bridgette lived only a couple of miles from his place, just across the line in Beverly Hills.

When he arrived at her deco style apartment complex, Bridgette was already on the sidewalk out front. Jeez! She was wearing skin-tight black leather pants, black cowboy boots with silver threading and a backless black leather vest. She was probably close to 5' 10", had straight black hair almost touching her shoulders, and had that half-grin she wore the first time they met. And him in Mabel. He double-parked, hopped out and opened the passenger door for her, closed it after she sat down and scooted back to the driver's side.

Bridgette was looking at him with a full smile now. She said, "Well, what are we waiting for?" Cliff lowered his head and shook it, mumbling to himself. "What did you say?", she asked. He took a deep breath, exhaled, and said, "Damn, you're a stone fox!"

"Why Jonesy. You say the nicest things!"

They started chatting about Lou Reed, the show and his car as he started off. "You went all out with this limousine tonight", she said. Cliff replied, "Let me introduce you to my other girl, Mabel. We've been together since university. We take pretty good care of each other. I felt bad about leaving her home on a Friday night."

Cliff drove west on Burton, then north on Doheny to Phyllis, then right on Carol where he found some open parking spots just below Sunset. They walked four short blocks to the Roxy, in to the bar for a round of drinks and across the floor to their seats. Their VIP seats were right next to the stage. Bridgette was floored. "These are our seats? How did you get these seats? Did you have to kill some one?"

Cliff smiled and said, "I have my ways. You like?"

She liked. The band opened with *Sweet Jane* from the Velvet Underground years. Lou Reed was only about six feet away from them. Cliff and Bridgette were both bopping away, standing with everyone else, the seats unused. The group played a couple more songs from the Velvet Underground, then moved through a bunch of songs from Reed's solo albums, ending with *I Want to Boogie with You* from The Bells album. The band had been on tour for quite a while and they were really tight. They sounded great, and the fans were going wild. An encore was not expected, but the crowd was so loud and demanding that they came out again, and finished with *Walk on the Wild Side* and *Heroin*. Even after the band left, the lights went up and the crowd started filing out, you could still feel the energy in the air.

Out on Sunset, it had cooled down and a breeze was up. Cliff saw Bridgette grab her upper arms and he quickly wrapped his tanker jacket around her shoulders. "You're ready for battle now", he joked as they walked arm-in-arm back to his car. It only took a few minutes to roll down the hill back to Arnaz Drive. He dropped a parallel park in an empty spot in from of her building, then hopped out and around to open the passenger door for her. "You're quite the old-fashioned gentleman, opening doors and stuff for me. What if I'm a liberated woman and want to take care of myself?" Cliff mumbled something about the car doors sometimes being difficult to open when he realized her eyes were sparkling and there was that grin.

He walked her to the door, took her hands and was getting ready to kiss her when she asked, "Want to come up for a bit?"

Seven

When they reached Bridgette's apartment on the third floor, she keyed open the door, let them both in and locked it back up. "Five second tour", she said. "This is the living room, that is the kitchen and back there is my bath and bedroom. Now you figure out my stereo and get something spinning on the turntable while I go touch up."

No touch up needed, he thought as he began flipping through her LP's. He found what he expected to find, put on *Ziggy Stardust* and wandered into the kitchen to check it out. "Oh Jonesy", he heard over the music, so he walked back into the living room. "In here", she called from the bedroom.

Cliff pushed open the door to the bedroom and in the half-light saw Bridgette sitting on the end of her bed. She kicked her feet straight out and said "Help me lose these boots." He grabbed first the left then the right heel and pulled them straight off her feet, turned around and set them next to her dresser. As he turned back to her, she was laying flat on her back. "Now these leathers", she said. Cliff's head was buzzing as he grabbed the cuffs and eased them over her ankles. The leathers came off slowly and he turned to place them with the boots. When he turned back around, Bridgette was on her feet and threw her arms around his neck. As their lips met, she leaned back a little and they tumbled onto the bed, Cliff's arms around her waist.

After a few minutes of kissing that left Cliff dizzy, he carefully extracted his arms and pushed himself up above her. He grinned as he moved down to unbutton her leather vest. Bridgette had grabbed his shirt and pulled it over his head. He pulled his arms out and carefully unbuttoned her vest. His head leaned down as he said, "Please introduce me to your friends." Bridgette laughed, grabbed his hair and mashed his face into her breasts.

After introducing himself to her fabulous breasts, Cliff started to slowly kiss his way down to her belly. When his tongue slipped into her navel he felt a shudder. As he kissed his way south, the shuddering became shaking. He went in with his lips to hers, then with his tongue flickering lightly across her little man in the boat, who seemed happy for him to be there. Soon, she was wet enough for him to slide a few fingers in and begin his rhythm. Slow, gentle, with occasional pauses that were met with load groans. Bridgette's shaking became violent, her hands were tearing at his hair, and finally a loud gasp and the shaking became convulsions. Cliff whispered "shark in the boat" as he eased off and slowed down his stroking, then slid up and put his arms around her. As Bridgette held him tight he could feel her heart still pounding and her breath still ragged. She was wet with sweat as he kissed her face.

After a while she calmed down and said to Cliff, "You bastard! How did you know how to do that? You're just a boy. You shouldn't know that stuff yet." Cliff chuckled and asked, "Boy?", as she pushed him off of her and sat up in the bed. She looked at him with that killer grin, tapped him on the nose with her index finger and said with a smile, "It's my turn now, boy!"

Eight

They awoke the next morning in a tangle of bed sheets, arms and legs. The process of untangling led to a morning love session, and the shower afterwards led to more fun. Eventually clothed and sipping coffee in Bridgette's kitchen she asked him, "So Jonesy, how old are you after all?

He smiled. "Twenty-four".

"And when did that happen?"

"A couple of months ago."

"That figures. I'm going to have to peel you like an onion to figure you out. But now I've got to throw you out or we'll be rutting all day. And I have to get some work done."

After a long embrace, Cliff was out the door and headed to the stairs. He heard, "Don't be a stranger..." and the door closed.

Nine

It took Cliff Jones only a few minutes to get home in the light Saturday traffic. When he got into his apartment, he lay down on the sofa and stared up at the ceiling. He had thoughts and feelings about Bridgette he had never experienced before. They had been so comfortable and easy together. There had been no stress or anxiety between them, there was just fun and enjoyment of each other. Is that what you call love when you are thinking about her constantly? He wanted to stay with her and he thought she might feel the same way, but they both had our own lives and had to live them. Everything seemed to have changed overnight. Even his apartment felt a little different than when he left last night. He felt a bit confused.

He changed into shorts, a tee and court shoes, then headed out the door to find a pick-up basketball game at the park. After a couple of hours of ball, he was beginning to feel a little more normal. This was what he did on Saturdays. When they were done with ball, Cliff went over to El Coyote with some of the other ballers. They drank some Coronas and ate tacos, watched some sports news on the TV and chattered about the Dodgers.

Back at his apartment he called Cy to see what was up on this Saturday night. It turns out the guys were all cramming for finals. "We haven't been studying much lately. The news from home is very bad and Shah had to go to the Bahamas last month. We don't think he will be able to stay there very long, either. That Khoumaini is started to execute anyone who was part of the government. They just killed Hovieda. He was Shah's Prime Minister in the early 60's when we were kids. But now, he was just a nice old man. This is getting crazy."

Cliff asked, "Are you going to be able to graduate and get your degrees? Did you get a new car yet?"

Cy replied, "Yeah, we're OK. It's only a month until graduation and tuition is all paid up. We're pretty much laying low now, and studying our asses off, so we don't need a car right now."

"What are you are going to do next?"

"We've gotta have a graduation party, right?"

Cliff said, "Okay. I'm looking forward to that party. And I think that '65 Oldsmobile is still available."

This time, Cy just laughed, "See you later man!"

So, it was going to be a quiet weekend. But what was going on in his apartment? Everything seemed to be where it should be, but then it wasn't really. Must be love, why he couldn't think straight, he chuckled to himself.

Ten

Sunday, May 6th Cliff Jones awakened early, feeling restless and lonely. He could still see Bridgette, feel her, taste her; he was obsessed. He planned a walk up to the Farmer's Market for some breakfast, then shopping. A reprise of how he met her, he thought. Then maybe a movie in the afternoon to distract him, take his mind off her for a little while. Cloudy weather today, and cool. Good day for a brisk walk. It would clear his head. He dressed quickly and got moving.

Cliff walked up the block and turned west on Wilshire, on the south side. He looked across to the tar pits and the art museum. They might be a good distraction later on. Sunday morning, Wilshire traffic was quiet. Only one person was on the sidewalk ahead of him. Walking briskly, Cliff was catching up. Fairfax was half a block ahead when the pedestrian turned around. Cliff felt his veins turn to ice. He knew the man! Medium build, dark hair, Member's Only jacket. It had been five years ago, but Cliff remembered him like yesterday. The undercover cops at his door, trying to buy pot! He froze. Before he could move, could even think, he heard a voice behind him, "Clifford Jones!".

Cliff spun around and the twin was there. Medium build, black hair, Member's Only jacket. What was happening? What had he done? His brain was spinning. Fear! Fight? Two on one, no way. Flight? On the south side, the building ran the length of the block. The only way open was to run out into the street, cross Wilshire and try to lose them in the park. The twin was holding out what looked like a badge and calling out "special agents!"

They must have realized he was going to run when they stopped approaching him and called out, "You're not under arrest! We just want to talk with you." As Cliff stood there, crouched down, ready to run, feeling like a frightened rabbit, a black limousine slid to the curb, effectively cutting off his escape route into the street. The back door opened and a voice called, "Cliff, please get in. And close the door." Was there a choice? As he cautiously stepped into the back seat and pulled the door closed behind him, he saw a figure sitting on the other side of the seat. Government/military short haircut, fairly fit, expensive suit, tie, maybe forty years old. The man leaned forward, rapped twice on the closed glass slider separating the rear compartment, and the vehicle slid slowly away from the curb.

It was quiet for a minute. Cliff and the man stared, sizing up each other. Cliff was thinking fast. Not under arrest. He had done nothing to warrant arrest, at least not in a while. Why wait so long? Did this have anything to do with the times he thought he saw that car following him, why he felt something weird happened in his apartment? Cliff spoke first, tensely, "Who are you? Why the hell am I here?"

Eleven

"Cliff, my name is Charles Wentworth. I am with the U.S. Department of State Office of Security. We call ourselves "SY" for short. Those two men you just met are my Special Agents. I wanted to talk with you today because we need your help."

"What if I don't want to help you?" said Cliff.

"Well, you don't really have a choice. We would like this to be a friendly relationship, and would rather not have to coerce your cooperation."

Cliff felt a chill. "If you had anything on me, you would have arrested me already. Five years ago those same two agents came to my home and tried to buy pot. Just like today, they were dressed like undercover cops. They got nothing on me. I think your guys have been following me for a couple of months, and now I have a bad feeling you broke into my apartment and tossed it on Friday night. There is nothing to find in my apartment, but even if there was, you had no warrant."

"You are pretty observant for a civilian. And my guys could do a better job of going undercover. Maybe you could help us with that, too..."

"But Cliff, we aren't the police, we aren't going to arrest you, and you are right that we never had enough evidence to turn you over to the cops. That was never the point, anyway. We just needed to be sure you weren't going to get our Princes in trouble. But we do know some things that might be embarrassing and damaging to your career and relationships. The concept is that in gratitude for your assistance, the State Department would make the skeletons in your closet, shall we say, go away?"

There is was. The blackmail. Those undercover agents in their Member's Only jackets, peeking through windows, taking photos: Him. Bongs. Pipes. Joints. Smoking. Drinking. Partying. Nothing that would hold up in court, but if they showed the photos around he could lose his job...

Cliff was still suspicious, not knowing if this man could be trusted. And, what would he have to do? "OK, Mr. Wentworth, I understand why I don't have a choice. I could see us helping each other if I knew a little more about what you need."

"I knew you were an intelligent and reasonable young man and you would want to help us," said Wentworth, blowing smoke up his ass. "You should feel good about helping both your country and your friends. I am guessing that I am not keeping you from anything pressing today? I hear you are recovering from a very busy Friday night. Now, I would like to tell you a story."

Cliff blushed deeply. How the fuck did he know...? Oh, right.

Twelve

Charles Wentworth expounded, "SY, the Office of Security is tasked with protecting diplomats and their families. Overseas, we team up with the Marines to protect our embassies and our people in them. We fucked up majorly earlier this year when our Ambassador to Afghanistan was murdered. If there is any consolation, some of the powers that be have begun to notice us, and may give us some more resources in the future."

"Here in the States, we are charged with protecting foreign diplomats and their families. We have been allies with the Shah for decades now, and we keep an eye on his family members and diplomats who are here in the States. This includes your friends Cyrus, Kamran and Gholam. When they came here six years ago they were told to keep to themselves and not advertise their royal connections. They were to stay out of trouble with the law. They have a cousin who assaulted a cop up in Sacramento and spent two months in jail. Very embarrassing for the Shah. Had to disown the kid. That won't happen again. We don't have the resources to keep them under constant surveillance, so we chose those two agents because they have Iranian-looking features. We thought we had dressed them to look like students, and we had them visit the campus once or twice a week to see how the royals were doing."

"Your friends were staying low and not getting noticed. But they were partying a lot. We saw them drinking alcohol and smoking marijuana. And you were there. A lot. You may not know it but you are the only American they regularly associate with. And they don't mingle with any of the other Iranians either. We were sure that you were their drug dealer and you would all get caught some day. So we set up that sting at your apartment to catch you selling drugs. You surprised us when you got angry and sent them away. How could you know? And we came back later and searched your apartment and found no drugs at all. We are still puzzled about that. Did we miss something?" He gave Cliff a quizzical look. Cliff did not reply.

"And your friends are still partying loudly, drinking booze and smoking marijuana, which they are getting from somewhere, we don't know. But you all have stayed under the radar so far. We figured that they are rich, young men. They are going to go partying and have a good time somewhere. So they do it with you. We used to think you were a bad influence on them, but maybe not? You seem to know how to avoid trouble. You got them away from the riot in Beverly Hills without being noticed. We've been following you since then to see what you are up to. And we searched your apartment Friday night, while you were occupied with your attractive lady friend. No marijuana, no cocaine, nothing illegal. And we checked with your employer. All of your drug tests are clean. Do you have anything you would like to say, Cliff?

"So I wasn't going crazy, thinking I was being followed, and that someone was messing with my head, rearranging my apartment."

Wentworth said, "No, you weren't going crazy."

"And my employer knows that the government is looking at my drug tests? What are they going to think is going on?"

Wentworth said, "We are a little more subtle than that. We requested that your bank provide drug test results for every employee in California."

Cliff took a deep breath. He could share a few things, but not everything. "OK, We party a lot. We drank a lot of booze and smoked a lot of pot, played the music loud and played drinking games. But they are good guys, no one got hurt, no one got in trouble, and we aren't doing anything illegal, except for the pot. Any everyone smokes pot these days. The guys have plenty of money and can buy whatever they want, but they don't like coke or other stuff. I have pretty much the same attitude. They have become my closest friends. I never tried to get them in trouble. All those years in school I never knew they were royalty, I thought they were just some rich kids. I didn't find out until after the riot."

"About the pot," Cliff continued, "You know it can be detected in the urine for up to thirty days. So thirty-one days before I graduated from 'SC back in '77, I quit cold turkey. So I could pass pee-tests. And keep my job, which I need. I've been clean ever since. The guys were surprised when I quit. I still drink and party with them, but no pot."

Charles Wentworth thought a moment then said, "That explains a lot. We need you to be clean. We couldn't associate with you if you were selling or using drugs. We were worried we didn't search your apartments hard enough." He fixed a tight smile.

Cliff said softly, " You could have searched for days. There was never anything to find there."

Wentworth started again: "Okay, now we both know your back story. Here is what will happen next. I am sure you know that Iran is falling apart. Whatever you hear our government saying about the situation, this is the reality: The Shah's regime is over, and he is dying of cancer. Khoumaini is in power now. We will eventually have to recognize his government, such as it is. We will pretend to making nice with him but he is an enemy of the US and is going to be a real problem. With the Shah and his regime out of power, we no longer have the mandate or resources to protect his family. We can drag it out for a while, but soon we will have to withdraw our protection. We hope the family will set up a government in exile and try to take back the country. Or some other group internally will grab power. But the American government cannot be seen helping any opposition groups. We can't even talk with them.

The Khoumaini government would point to any American contact with opposition groups as proof that they are just American puppets. We think many Iranians still think favorably of America, but we can't be seen interfering with their internal affairs."

"Cliff, here is your job: Continue to see your friends, the Princes, and keep a low profile. They will know that SY is no longer actively protecting them, but you will be their back door to the US government. After they finish school next month, we have to remove their protection. You will keep us posted on their activities, especially if they get involved with any opposition groups."

"Here is where it gets tricky. We know that the Iranians are sending hit squads around the world to kill off the Pahlavi family. That includes your friends. You will need to be vigilant. If you think that you all are being watched or followed, it won't be us any more. You will be in danger too. If you can identify a specific threat for us, we may be able to arrange some sort of response, but don't hold your breath. If it gets too dangerous for your friends we can talk about relocation and new identities, but that is time-consuming and difficult."

"Cliff, are you on board?"

Cliff just sat there, staring into space. "Um... I would really like to help my friends, especially if their lives are in danger. So, I am on board. No blackmail required. I would help out anyway. But I don't think I am qualified to do this kind of...of...spy work?"

Charles Wentworth smiled and said, "Don't worry about that. We will give you some special training. You will be much more confident in your abilities after the training. And Cliff, don't sell yourself short. I think you are a very smart guy who knows how to think fast. A drug dealer who couldn't be caught." He gave Cliff a knowing look and raised his eyebrows.

Cliff dropped his head and muttered, "Alleged drug dealer."

Charles Wentworth handed Cliff a business card. Cliff read: "Fred Alen, Federal Bureau of Investigation. What's this?"

"Fred is a friend of mine. He owes me a favor. He is also one of the FBI's best trainers. You will report to him at 8:00 AM for the next three Saturdays at the address written on the back of his card. Then, in a month, on Saturday June 2 at 8:00 AM, I will pick you up at the exact spot on Wilshire where we met today. Don't be late!"

Thirteen

The next week moved slowly for Cliff. He waited until Wednesday evening around 9:00PM to ring Bridgette, so as not to seem too clingy, but got no answer. Same result Thursday night. He wondered about the weekend training. Ever since the riot at their mansion, he thought the guys might be in some danger, but hit squads trying to assassinate them, wow!

Saturday morning found Cliff poking around a business park by the Long Beach Airport. He found the FBI address on a nondescript three story office building, parked and found the lobby door locked. He tried to peer in through the darkened glass and knocked on the door a few times. Finally a large security guard in a typical rent-a-cop uniform with gun on hip opened the door and asked "What do you want?"

"I'm supposed to meet Fred Alan here at 8AM."

The guard barked "Not here." and closed the door. Cliff frowned and sat down on the steps. And waited. About 8:30 AM another car pulled into the parking lot and a frumpy middle aged man got out. As he approached the door Cliff asked, "Are you Fred?"

The man looked him up and down and said, "You must be that kid Chuck sent over, Clete, or something like that?"

"It's Cliff."

"Well whatever, just follow me." This is a rough start, Cliff thought.

Fred knocked on the door and the security guard opened it immediately. "Good morning Mr. Alen." he said. "What brings you here on a Saturday?"

"Morning Gus. I'm paying off a favor. I'll be here the next couple of Saturdays giving this kid some training." said Fred.

"I'm Cliff. Cliff Jones." he said hopefully.

After passing through several locked doors with keys and codes, they rode a code-locked elevator down into the basement of the building, walked down a hallway and entered a large, cool and dark room. As the door slammed behind them, Fred hit the lights and Cliff realized they were in a shooting range. There were a variety of firearms laid out at different stations, each with a paper target of a human some distance down the range.

"I don't know why Chuck wants a kid like you to get this training." said Fred. "Chuck said you won't be issued a gun, or even be an employee. I don't know why he wants you to be familiar with guns."

Cliff knew why. He wondered if Wentworth knew that Cy had a gun. Cliff had to keep Cy from firing that gun, or it would bring on all sorts of unwanted attention. On the other hand, Cy might have no choice but to use his gun. This was getting real.

Cliff was quiet for a moment. "I've never handled a gun before. I guess if I knew how to load, fire, then unload, I would have a better idea of what to do if someone points one at me. You know, like should I run, or hide?"

"Ha! You're funny, kid! You do know that bullets run faster than people. Only Superman can outrun a bullet. But some guns take longer to load, point and shoot than others. And some guns don't shoot very far. Let's see what you can learn."

Fred started a hands-on lecture for Cliff, going down the row of guns. He explained the make and model, bullet size and capacity, range and accuracy of each one. Cliff learned the location of the safety on guns that had them. He learned to unload each gun, then reload. He handled revolvers, semi-automatic pistols, rifles, shotguns. "You'll do some shooting after I finish explaining all this. Even with our protective headgear, we won't be able to hear each other after the first shots."

Cliff knew he would never remember all these names and details, but he associated the similar type of weapons together in his mind and focused on how to load and unload. He figured that the only way he was going to touch a gun out there was if he took it from someone. That was not a good thought.

Eventually, they donned ear protection and began shooting the weapons. Some were easier than others to fire. Cliff hit most of the targets, some better than others. He decided that the best guns for him were the shotguns. He just pointed, pulled the trigger and the target became confetti.

Afterwards, Cliff helped Fred clean up and store everything away. "Thanks for helping me clean up, kid. Now I'll be able to get home in time for the game. Dodgers have finally won five in a row and they have the Expos at home tonight."

"See you next Saturday, kid. 8:00 AM sharp...ish!"

Fourteen

It was another uneventful week at work for Cliff. He finally caught Bridgette at home on Tuesday evening.

"Hi Bridgette, how are you doing?"

"Hiya Jonesy, its nice to hear from you. It's been a while."

"Well, I tried calling you a few times last week, but you were out. I didn't want to be a pest."

"You're not a pest, lover boy. I like to hear your voice."

"I miss you too, but I guess you are really busy. I would love to get together soon."

"Me too. But I am just so busy. This is the first time I've been home before midnight in a week."

"Girl's gotta eat sometime. Can we get together for dinner?...lunch?...breakfast? I'll call Lou Reed. Whatever. You tell me when and I'll be there."

"Jonesy, you crack me up. You know, I never asked if you like me calling you Jonesy?"

"You can call me anything you like. And I do have a serious jones for you, serious..."

"Mmmmmm! We'll have to work on that. But I am so busy with a project this month that I don't have any time free. But call me next week. Just so I can hear your voice."

"OK, will do!" said Cliff.

"Good night, Jonesy..."

Fifteen

Saturday, May 19th at 8:00 AM, Cliff was sitting in the parking lot at the FBI office, waiting for Fred Alen to show up. This time, Fred arrived at 8:15AM, and had a smile for Cliff as they entered the lobby. "Sorry, I can't blame traffic for being late, being a Saturday..." Cliff laughed, appreciating the acknowledgment.

"Morning Gus. Remember me?", asked Cliff of the security guard. Then to Fred, "What's up for today, boss?"

"Well, we'll be reviewing something else we hope you never need to use. Today is all about what we call drops. Dead drops allow people to communicate without ever meeting. Live drops are similar, but include a brief encounter. Let's make some coffee because the lecture part is pretty boring."

After getting their coffees, Fred led Cliff to a small conference room. They got comfortable, then Fred stood at a whiteboard.

"Here goes: A dead drop is a place two people agree to use as a place to exchange information, like notes, blueprints, formulae, plans, photos, you name it. Sounds simple, but you need to have a place that is secure. You can't have some stranger accidentally find your drop and throw away your critical plans, thinking they are junk. You can't have your adversaries follow you to the drop and then take your information. But you must be able to get to the drop quickly and un-noticed. Do you get the idea?"

"So Cliff, tell me somewhere that might be a good place for a drop?"

"Hmm, how about under a toilet cover?"

"That's a good idea. That reminds that a waterproof package is usually a good idea. And if your package is thin enough it could go behind the toilet tank."

"Or how about behind a radiator?" asked Cliff, "if it's not sensitive to heat."

"You're getting the idea. Anywhere that's not obvious," said Fred. "Can you go out in the woods and look in a knot hole while you are wearing a suit? Can you get into your drop and get away with no one paying attention to you?"

"Now for signals. These are easier to hide, in plain sight. When you fill the drop box, you leave a mark somewhere that you have agreed on. Usually a chalk mark on a sign is enough, anything so slightly changed that only your partner will notice. Once the exchange is complete, your partner leaves some signal so that you know the drop is complete. "

"The advantage of the dead drop, if you do it right, is that no one can connect the two people together because they are never seen together. And the signals minimize the number of visits to the drop."

"OK, here is the classic live drop: Person one goes into a coffee shop, sits down and puts their newspaper on the table. Person two comes in next, and asks to share the table. They put their newspapers next to each other's. Partner one then picks up Partner two's paper and leaves."

"They must have the same newspaper. Sometimes they exchange code words if the two don't know each other, or to tell whether the coast is clear or not."

"The advantage of the live drop is that the information is positively transferred. There is no risk of it being lost or stolen. The disadvantage is that both parties could be seen together. Some ways to get around that are having the transfer in a crowded, busy place. The information is quickly dropped into a shopping bag or pocket."

After all this, Fred said, "Let's stretch our legs." Once outside, Fred pointed to the corner of the building. "In the hundred-foot square area from the corner of the building, including the little garden, the lawn and the parking lot is a drop box. See if you can find it. You will not have to dig. You have ten minutes."

Cliff started poking around while Fred lit a cigarette. Cliff realized as an exercise, the drop would be hidden in plain site. He started examining the garden very closely. After five minutes or so, Fred said "I'm lighting another smoke. You should be able to find it before I'm finished."

Cliff realized the garden couldn't be searched that quickly, but where? The lawn would require digging to find something. The building was smooth, with no crannies to hide anything. That left the parking lot. Flat. Except for the concrete bumpers at the top of each parking spot. When Cliff stepped into the parking lot, he saw Fred smile. The third bumper from the corner had a little gleam under it, which turned out to be a sandwich bag with some Dodger tickets in it.

Fred said, "Chuck gave me the tickets. He said they are yours if you found them. They were mine if you didn't. I wasn't expecting much from you when we started last week. But I'm impressed. You're doing all right."

"Chuck wants you to understand the importance of secure communications. But I want you to stay away from drops. Almost always, both parties get caught. And back in the USSR, you know what that means."

"Anyway, see you next Saturday. It will definitely be more fun than today."

Sixteen

The next week was slow again at work. Gas lines were long, so people were staying home, maybe hoarding gas for the upcoming holiday weekend. Cliff Jones had plenty of time to think about his training sessions. Fred had told him that he wasn't an agent, just a civilian employee, normally a nine to five guy who ran training classes at the main FBI headquarters in the Federal Building in west LA. But Cliff was getting private lessons in a deserted office building on the weekend. Charles Wentworth was definitely trying to keep it secret.

The Dodger tickets were a nice perk. Friday night against the Reds, good rivalry. The box seats were just behind third, his favorite location in the stadium. Cliff had been trying to call Bridgette all week, but no answer. He had never asked before, but thought she would enjoy a baseball game. He was a little sad that he hadn't seen Bridgette since the beginning of the month and just talked with her the once. He was jonesing for her, definitely, but he really enjoyed just hanging out with her. They had broken the ice quickly on that first date at Du Pars and already knew a lot about each other.

Cliff hadn't seen his Persian friends either, with their cramming for final exams. He had given them space to get their work done, but he had four tickets and a ball game would be a fun break, not an all-night party. And he had his final training session with Fred the next morning anyway.

Cy answered right away when Cliff called. "Hey man, I'm glad you called. Our heads are spinning with all this studying, but we are finally catching up. We had pretty much ditched school for the last few months because of all this shit going down. But we might as well complete these degrees that we have paid for, even if we don't know what comes next".

Cliff said, "I'm glad to hear that you're gonna get those degrees.

How about a little break from studying to clear your heads?"

"Man, I would love to have one of our crazy all-night parties but our heads would be fucked up for days. We are doing good, but we have to keep studying."

"No, no, I've got something fun, but low key." Cliff said. "I've got four box seats for the Dodgers game tomorrow night. Reserved parking up front and seats right behind the dugout."

"That baseball of yours is a boring sport, the players just stand around most of the time."

Cliff said, "Maybe on TV. But have you ever seen a live game? It's much better. Lots going on. The crowd will be excited, there are pretty girls and the beer is cold. I know you would like it. And you can leave whenever you want."

Cy said, "You're tempting me man. But I don't have my car yet."

"Yet?" exclaimed Cliff. "You're getting a car? Great news! What kind?"

"It's a graduation present...if I graduate. I'm keeping it secret for now, but I guarantee you man-it is not a fucking beat up 1965 Oldsmobile station wagon!"

Cliff laughed at that. "It's OK, I can pick you up with Mabel. There is only one parking pass anyway. Tell the guys to be ready at 5:30 tomorrow."

Seventeen

Friday was busy at the bank with the usual paycheck cashing crowd and the Memorial Day holiday on Monday. Mid-afternoon, Cliff crossed the aisle from his loan desk to the Operations side. He was well liked over there because he was not too proud to remember his days as a teller, and helped out there when it was needed.

Everyone was excited to have a three-day weekend and most of the cash drawers were balanced and closed fast. Cliff used his particular skill to do sums in his head. He could do them faster than most people on calculators. The two tellers having trouble were grateful to Cliff for figuring out their issues and closing their drawers by 5:00 PM, so everyone could leave. Nobody wanted to be that last teller struggling to close when everyone else was ready to leave, especially on a Friday, and especially on a holiday.

Chris Noble caught Cliff slipping out in casual clothes. "Hot date tonight?!" he asked.

"I wish," said Cliff. "But not all bad either. Box seats for the game tonight!"

Luckily, traffic was still light. There were lines into the street at every gas station, but Cliff had filled up two nights earlier. He slipped down Mariposa to 8th Street to avoid Wilshire, then south on Vermont all the way to Exposition. East on Exposition, a quick right on Flower, u-turn in the street and he was at Garret Gardens with minutes to spare.

He honked and the guys were down the stairs in no time. Cliff realized they were probably suffering from cabin fever. The piles of pizza boxes visible in the kitchen window confirmed his hunch. Cy as usual cried, "Shotgun!" and jumped in front next to Cliff, with Goalie sitting behind him. Cliff said, "Hey Kammy, don't forget to slam your door or it will fly open on our first left turn."

Everyone was in high spirits. Cliff drove up to Exposition, turned right, and then left at Broadway. Kammy's door held, to everyone's amusement. He took almost-deserted Broadway all the way up to Ord, turned right and parked in front of Philippe the Original. "You guys been here before?" called Cliff as they all piled out. "You gotta get a French Dip. You'll like the lamb." "No eyeballs, though," he teased.

As they settled in with four lamb dips and four cold beers, Cliff explained, "This is the best sandwich in LA. Been here over seventy years. And the only food at Dodger Stadium is hot dogs and Cracker Jack."

They had a second round of beers and everyone was happy! Cliff drove them back to Broadway north, left on College, then the right turn jog to Stadium Way. Showing the parking pass, they were directed into Lot B, then right up to the stadium. They were waved into a numbered spot right at the entrance to the stadium. Valets checked their tickets, then escorted them to their seats. Cliff was thrilled: right behind the dugout, best seats in the house, same view the players had of the game.

Cy, Goalie and Kam were looking around, clearly impressed. Cy said, "I have never seen a stadium like this. Our stadiums at home are like your Coliseum, dirty and old. Look at this, everything is perfect, green grass, red dirt, clean seats, bright lights!" And when the game got going, it was a fan favorite. The Dodgers came out slugging, with seven homers and twenty hits, two brawls between the players and final score of 17 to 6. They took turns making beer runs. As promised by Cliff, there were lots of pretty girls in the seats and up at the concession stands. Kammy even tried Cracker Jack against Cliff's advice.

Driving home down deserted Broadway once again, Cy said:

"Cliff, that was very cool of you to take us to baseball. It's a great sport and fun to watch – in person. But I still won't be watching on TV."

The guys were quiet now, which gave Cliff an opportunity to ask, "So, how are things on campus? Is anyone harassing you guys or any of the other Persians? Is there any news from home that I don't see in the newspapers?"

Cy said, "It's pretty cool on campus. Nobody is bothering anyone else. The news from home is all bad. It's turning into a full-on civil war. None of the ethnics want to be under Khoumaini. Shah knew how to take care of them. He let them keep their own customs as long as they didn't cause trouble. Khoumaini is trying to make them do all that fundamentalist shit, and the Kurds and Arabs, they're not into that."

"What are you going to do after graduation?" asked Cliff. "You certainly can't go home now."

"You know, we haven't really thought about it with all this studying for finals. We don't know."

Cliff said, "It's really boring around campus in the summer – I know. I spent three summers there while you guys went home. Let me stick an idea in your heads. Why don't you move to the beach. Marina del Rey is pretty cool, laid back, lots of young people, pretty girls in bikinis, and a nice beach nearby. There are lots of bars, restaurants and stores you can walk to. Or Manhattan Beach a little further south. It's a little more laid back, but it is really hopping during the summer. Plus, they're both near LAX, in case you ever need to leave in a hurry. Just think about it."

Eighteen

Saturday, May 26, 8:00AM, at the FBI office in Long Beach, Cliff Jones had waved to Gus the security guard and was waiting on the steps for Fred Alen. Fred showed up at 8:15AM as before, but didn't get out of his car, just rolled down the window. "Hop in," he said, "I'll explain on the way." He jumped on the 405 north and then Harbor Freeway heading towards downtown LA. "We were going to do this in Long Beach, but with the gas crisis, there is not enough traffic there, so we're going to LA. You are going to be introduced to surveillance and counter-surveillance today. This training usually takes months, so you are getting the crash course. We will show you how to tell if someone is following you, and how to follow someone without being seen."

"Fred, I wanna thank you for the tickets. You could have put a business card in that baggie instead. I never would have known. By the way, it was a great game." said Cliff.

Fred chuckled. "I know I could have kept the tickets. I ended up watching at home instead. You deserved them though. No way you are going to be fully prepared for what's out there, but I've been impressed how quickly you pick up on this stuff. You should know I didn't want to do this at first and Chuck had to seriously twist my arm to make me. I don't know exactly what Chuck is doing with you, but I have a rough idea. My conscience will feel better if what I'm teaching you saves your ass out there."

"At exactly 9:00 AM, I am going to drop you at the corner of 6th and Los Angeles Streets. You are to walk around the block up to 5th Street and over to Maple Avenue and back down to 6th. There will be ten people following you. There will be hundreds of pedestrians and vehicles because it is Saturday and that block is all small wholesale and retail markets. Your job is to identify those ten trackers to me when I pick you up at the same corner in exactly one hour, 10:00AM."

Fred added, "Some ideas for you. You can look in the reflection of a store window to see if the same person is still following you. Walk ahead fast, then turn around. See if someone else stops with you. You can jaywalk to see if someone follows, but stay on the block. You can go into the shops, pretend to shop and scoot out. You're pretty smart. You'll figure out other ways to spot your trackers."

At 9:00AM, Cliff got out of the car and started walking up Los Angeles Street. He soon noticed a man in a red ball cap who seemed to be following him. He walked fast, turned around and... no red ball cap. He walked back the other way and saw a man turn and walk away from him. Red ball cap in the rear pants pocket. Got one! This is kind of fun. Of course, if the followers were actually trying to kill him, no fun at all.

Cliff caught eight more followers in the next half hour, but then it got tough. He finally caught number ten by pretending to shop in a store, then ran out fast and immediately into the store next door. The follower practically knocked him over. Cliff was walking slowly back toward his rendezvous when he saw someone following him, reflected in a store window. A woman with a shopping bag, wearing a plaid jacket and big floppy hat. He turned the corner, then reversed and went back. He saw a woman with no jacket or hat, but carrying an overstuffed shopping bag. He walked by her, then turned his head back without stopping. There was something plaid in the shopping bag. Number Eleven!?

Back in Fred's car at 10:00AM, Cliff recounted his eleven trackers. "Did I expose someone else by accident?"

Fred laughed. "The woman you exposed as your second tracker is actually one of our better street people. She was so embarrassed you found her so quickly that she put on a different disguise and went out again! So, nice job. And that's a good lesson: Just because you spotted someone watching you, don't stop looking. There could be multiple people following you."

"Our next exercise puts you behind the wheel, Cliff. I will be in the passenger seat giving you advice. At exactly 10:30AM a 1978 desert tan Ford Fairmont will leave 5th Street, heading north on Wall Street. You will be parked facing north on Wall Street, about half a block below 5th Street. You job is to follow that car without being seen. If the driver spots you as his tracker, he will park and get out, and wave hi! Otherwise he will keep driving until 11:00AM. The only rules of this exercise are to stay north of 6th Street, in the area bordered by the 110 and 101 freeways."

At 10:30AM, Cliff could see the tan Fairmont pull into traffic and drive north. Fred said, "Now you have to wait until there are a few cars between you or you'll be spotted right away."

Cliff took off behind the Fairmont, keeping several cars between them. The driver was making random turns, left and right, occasionally speeding up, then slowing down. Cliff learned not to speed up too quickly and almost lost the driver twice. After about twenty minutes, Cliff was following the driver east on 3rd Street. He knew he was getting close to the end of 3rd, at the railroad tracks, when the driver sped up and made a hard right into a driveway. Cliff should have kept going straight and stopped further down 3rd, watching his rear view. Instead, the adrenaline got to him and he followed, realizing immediately it was a dead end. The driver had quickly u-turned and was stopped and waving as Cliff flew by into the dead end.

Cliff and Fred were sitting at a counter in the Grand Central Market on Broadway, having lunch and reviewing the morning's exercises. "From what Chuck told me, today's training might be the most valuable. Whether you are hiding or seeking, you need to be calm and plan a few steps ahead, like chess."

"Think about this: If someone is following and they want to

hurt you, they won't be evasive. They'll just go and get you. So if the follower is being evasive, you might let them follow you. They want to know where you're going. They don't know you have training, but if you use evasive tactics, they will know you've been trained, and they will know you are on to them. So maybe you just lead them away from your planned destination and go into a busy crowded place where there will be potential witnesses."

"And if you are the follower, better to lose your target than let them know they are being followed. You learned that today in the car. If you don't spook them, maybe you can find and follow them another day."

They drove back to the FBI lot, mostly in silence. Too many things were spinning in Cliff's head to form specific questions. As they got closer to the lot, they chatted about the Dodgers. They were playing the Reds again this afternoon. Would they win their eighth in a row? Fred was going to watch at home from the sofa, with a few beers. Cliff thought he might walk over to Tom Bergin's on Fairfax and watch from the bar with a corned beef sandwich.

As they parted in the parking lot, Fred asked, "Have you ever thought of becoming an FBI Agent? You would do well. And don't lose my business card. Call if you need advice."

As they shook hands, Fred said "Good luck. You'll need it."

Nineteen

Saturday, May 26, 8:15 AM, Special Agent B.C. Evans was about to enter the parking lot at the FBI office in Long Beach. There was a car sliding out the exit with two persons in it. The driver looked like Fred Alen. Odd, Fred usually worked Monday to Friday in the main office in West L.A. Being a civilian employee he didn't do crazy long hours and weekend like the Special Agents did. What was he doing here?

A knock on the front door and Gus the security guard opened it. "Good morning Special Agent. What brings you here on a Saturday morning?"

Evans answered, "Some raw data for my current assignment arrived here from the border crossings. It will take a couple of weeks before it gets into our computers, and I can't wait that long. So I will be up in the intake room, pouring over the details."

"Say, was that Fred Alen I saw leaving the parking lot?"

Gus answered, "Right you are. Fred has been training a young guy for the last few Saturdays. Fred seemed pretty pissed off to lose his Saturdays at first, but now he seems to be warming up to the kid. And this kid even tried to suck up to me."

"Interesting! Anyway, would you ring up to me if Fred comes back?

"Sure thing, Boss!"

Twenty

Special Agent Evans got to work in the intake room and the hours flew by. Nothing earthshaking in the new data, but there was enough to keep the investigation moving forward. Mid-afternoon, Gus called up to the intake room and stated, "Fred Alen is in the parking lot." Evans went rapidly down the stairs to the lobby, a quick "Thanks, Gus" and stepped out the front door onto the top step.

Fred looked up, smiled and said "Good afternoon Special Agent Evans! To what do I owe this honor?"

Evans said, "Usually I'm the only one working these crazy weekend hours. What brings you here?

Fred said, "I was paying back a favor I owed to Chuck Wentworth over at SY, State Department. He wanted me to give this young guy, Cliff Jones, some experience in basic tradecraft."

"You mean like the training I had a few years ago? Evans asked. "You dropped us downtown and gave us an hour to find ten people tracking us? And we figured you only had six or seven trackers out there, just to confuse us, because no one ever found more than five or six." Evans was smiling now. "So how many trackers did your trainee find?

"Eleven." said Fred flatly.

Evans' smile was gone. "Oh my..."

"The kid is really good. Eyes in the back of his head. I even tried to recruit him for the FBI," said Fred. "Told him he'd be a great SA. But I'm done here, the debt is paid off, and the Dodgers are playing now. I'm outta here! Nice to see you."

Evans was confused now. What was State doing, using the FBI to train Cliff Jones? Back in the intake room was a terminal coupled into the FBI main frame. There was nothing about Jones in the FBI database. A search in State Department personnel for "Cliff Jones" was also fruitless. "Wentworth" rang a bell. A directory search revealed that Charles Wentworth worked for State Department security, SY, out of the Federal Building in west LA. Neighbors! Probably a few flights up. But why Cliff Jones?

Evans returned to work reviewing the raw data from Immigration. It was after nine by the time it was done. Driving home, there was time to ponder Fred Alen, Cliff Jones and Charles Wentworth. What the hell was going on?

Twenty-one

The next morning, after an unsettled night, Special Agent Bridget Evans decided what she had to do with Cliff Jones. And he made it easier by ringing her phone at 9:00 AM. She suspected he had been calling regularly while she was working late.

"Hi Bridgette. I can't ever catch you at home in the evenings. So I hope I didn't wake you up."

"Oh, Cliff, no, no. You didn't wake me. And I'm glad you called."

"Oh good. I am hoping you could take a break from your studies and hang out. It's Memorial Day weekend and everyone else has the day off tomorrow. What do you say?"

He's such a puppy dog, Bridgette thought. This is making it so much easier. "You know, I would like to take the day off tomorrow. And I want to cook a nice dinner for you tonight. So... why don't you knock on my door around six tonight, with a nice bottle of wine in your hand."

Cliff was thrilled. "For sure, I'll be there!"

"Oh, and bring your toothbrush," said Bridgette as she hung up.

Bridgette smiled to herself. She thought that Cliff was way too young for her, but he kept surprising her in a good way, both in and out of bed. And so what? She didn't have any other relationship going on, and this was getting to be a lot of fun. So tonight she would begin to peel the onion that was Cliff and she would know more about what he was up to. She was a little nervous about interrogating him. She was known to be a tough interrogator. Maybe she could go a little easier than normal with him. If he didn't freak out and run away when she revealed that she was actually a Special Agent, they could enjoy the rest of the evening together. Very enjoyable, she hoped.

Twenty-two

Cliff Jones was excited. He had not been sure if Bridgette was trying to push him away by being unavailable so much of the time, but felt much better now. He guessed that they might have more mind-blowing sex, like before, but also looked forward to just hanging out tomorrow, brunch, beach or whatever.

After playing basketball over at the park, Cliff drove to Trader Joe's, squeezed his car into the incredibly tiny parking lot, and walked in. What an interesting selection of wine, and, of course, once a wine was gone, it never came back. One of the sales associates he knew in the wine department helped him chose a nice French Chablis. Something that would go with a variety of foods. Next stop was at the Farmers Market to get a bouquet of flowers, not too big, but not too small.

Cliff got himself ready for tonight and tomorrow with a shave and shower, then packed a bag with a change of clothes for tomorrow. He had some fun ideas for them tomorrow and wanted to be ready. He was out the door and loaded the wine, flowers and overnight bag into Mabel at about ten minutes before six. After the short drive to Arnaz Drive he found an open parking spot near Bridgette's apartment, and, leaving the overnight bag in the trunk, carried everything else upstairs. No sign of Wentworth's agents tonight, he thought. He walked to her door and knocked.

The door opened and there stood Bridgette, beautiful as always. She was wearing a little pair of terrycloth drawstring shorts, a tube top and a smile.

Twenty-three

"Stop drooling!" she commanded. Bridgette drew Cliff inside and closed and latched the door. She leaned up and gave him a big smack on the lips, leaned back, smiled and said, "Flowers! Jonesy! How sweet. And there's the wine, as requested. Give me the flowers and you get that wine opened for us."

Bridgette dropped the flowers into a vase and Cliff opened the wine, found some wine glasses and poured two. Bridgette asked him to put on some music while she finished up the dinner. Cliff put KKGO on the FM radio, figuring a little jazz would be appropriate, and no need to flip LP's. He wandered back into the kitchen and picked up his wine glass. He was staring again, and starting to make a little small talk when he noticed that Bridgette seemed a little off, like she was preoccupied or agitated, and he asked her, "Bridge, is everything OK? You seem to be a little agitated."

She turned around and looked at him, eyes a little wary. "I was going to do this later, but I can't wait. I have something I have to get off my chest."

"I don't suppose it's that tube top, is it?", he joked.

She smiled, shook her head and said, "You!"

She said softly, "Put down your glass." and then took his hands.

"I have a confession to make." She paused. "I am not really a paralegal, and I am not studying for a J.D. Degree." Bridgette paused. Cliff was silent, slightly puzzled. She said, "I already have my J.D. and I am a Special Agent with the FBI."

Now Cliff looked stunned. After a moment of silence Bridgette said, "I didn't like lying to you, but the Agency's policy is that Agents should not reveal ourselves when we are off-duty. So they give us a make-believe occupation to use in our daily routine.

That's why I haven't told you."

Cliff spoke slowly, drawing out his words one-by-one, "You're FBI?...The FBI?...G-men...no, G-woman?...badge?...gun?...handcuffs?...all that?"

"Yes, all of that." she answered softly. "What are you thinking?"

Cliff smiled a little half-smile and shook his head. Almost to himself he said, "I'm dating a cop. I can't believe I'm dating a cop!"

"Is there something wrong with that?", Bridgette asked with a look of mock horror.

Now Cliff laughed out loud. "I never thought I would date a cop. Those guys in blue that I keep running into are not nearly as fun or beautiful as you."

"Are we good then?", she asked, and he replied, "We've always been more than good."

Bridgette wrapped him up in a hug, which he joined. "I was so worried that you wouldn't be able to handle it," she said into his shoulder. "It's actually kind of a turn on," he said. She looked up and he began to kiss her on the lips. It lasted a few minutes, long enough to get them both warm. She gently pushed him back, saying "Whoa there big fella...I've got to feed you first."

Bridgette dropped some butter in a pan, and when it was sizzling, pulled two brook trout from the refrigerator and placed them skin up in the butter. After sizzling for a few minutes she flipped them, and squeezed a lemon over them. Then there was a sprinkling of slivered almonds and capers, and she slid the fillets on to the waiting plates and placed them on the table. Side Caesar salads came out of the fridge and Cliff topped up the glasses with wine.

"To surprise!", toasted Cliff.

"To surprise!", replied Bridgette. If he only knew, she thought. The first part, the confession, had gone well. We'll see how the interrogation goes.

The trout was fabulous and perfectly cooked. Bridgette basked in his praise. Cliff had said, "Your cooking skills are almost as big a surprise as the other surprise."

After a quick after-dinner cleanup, Cliff washing and Bridgette drying and putting away, they settled side by side on the living room sofa with the last of the wine. Cliff had his arm around her shoulder and she was resting her head against his neck. Something was nagging at Cliff and he finally knew what it was. "Bridge, why did you decide to tell me about the FBI now? I mean, it's your policy to keep it private."

"Since you asked, Cliff, I accidentally discovered your secret yesterday. Somehow, you are involved with both the State Department and the FBI."

Cliff was jolted into attention. No one knew...except Fred, Gus, Wentworth, who was it?

"How do you know.?...Who told you?...Then he guessed, "You know Fred?" When her eyes went big, he knew that was it. But how?

Bridgette told him, "Cliff, I normally work at our headquarters in the Federal building on the west side. But Saturday there was some data for me to review in the satellite office in Long Beach. Being a Saturday I figured the place would be deserted. But as I pulled into the parking lot yesterday morning, you were leaving with Fred. And there was a familiar looking old Nova in the back of the parking lot."

"Later in the day, when Fred returned, I buttonholed him. He told me that he was giving you some training to pay off a favor he owed to someone at the State Department named Wentworth. Fred is a civilian employee of the Agency, and works out of our headquarters, a Monday to Friday guy. Everyone knows Fred. We've all been in his classes. So how come you got private lessons on his day off, in a deserted location?"

Cliff sighed. "I think it was supposed to be a secret, but if Fred told you, I guess it doesn't matter any more."

Bridgette showed a small smile and said, "Just tell me your story. You can trust me."

"I want to trust you. I don't think I can trust Wentworth. Here goes. Sunday morning, the 6th of this month, I was walking down Wilshire by Fairfax when two plainclothes cops come at me from both sides. They were yelling "Special Agents" and waving badges. There is a building right on the sidewalk, no escape that way, so I had to run out into the street to get away. Just then, a big limo pulls to the curb, blocking my way. The back door opens, and a voice inside calls my name and tells me to get in. I was trapped anyway, so I got in. The cops slammed the door on me and the limo drove off."

"The guy in the limo is Charles Wentworth. He works for State Department security. They call themselves SY. He and his agents have been watching and protecting my Persian friends ever since they came here six years ago. But now that the Shah is out of power, the guys are not going to get any more protection from the State Department. So Wentworth wants me to keep an eye on my friends. And pass messages back and forth. And since they might be in danger from the Iranian death squads, Wentworth thought that I should get some training. So, there it is."

Bridgette thought that she wanted to "peel the onion" and learn

Cliff's secrets, but this was way more than she expected. "So who exactly are your friends? And why would you even consider doing this job? It sounds really dangerous. You could be killed!"

Cliff replied, "I've known these guys for almost six years and I thought they were just regular guys...well, just regular rich guys! When I helped them get away from the riot, I found out they are the Shah's nephews. They are the Princes of Persia! And that means they are in danger. I am their only American friend. They don't hang out with other Persians, either, except for their family, for obvious reasons. I would help them anyway because they are my best friends. But Wentworth told me I don't have a choice."

This is getting really crazy, thought Bridgette. "Why wouldn't you have a choice about such a dangerous job?"

Cliff said, "Wentworth told me that they could release some information that would hurt my career and relationships. But if I cooperated, he could make it go away forever."

"Blackmail!, she exclaimed. He nodded. "And wait, What riot?"

"They were at the Beverly Hills mansion with their aunt and the Shah's mother, having a New Years party. Their aunt likes to hold these movie screenings for her friends and family. Then the riot started and Cy's car was burned and they had no way home because all of the SY had left with the aunt and queen. They couldn't go out because of all the press there, you know, taking photos. And there were cops roaming around looking for Iranians. They would have been arrested and identified. So they called me and I drove up there and sneaked them out the back way. That's when I realized that the auntie they talk about is the Shah's sister, the one with that huge mansion in Beverly Hills."

"Wow! You're already involved in all this. What is Wentworth using to blackmail you?" asked Bridgette.

"Do you really want to know? Will you still love me?"

"Cliff, I might know a little more than you think. You're not going to be in trouble with me. In fact, I might be able to help you out."

"I really hope so. SY has also been watching me for the last six years because I was hanging out with the guys a lot. When we hung out, we would party, play loud music and drink lots of booze. We smoked a lot of pot, too, and played drinking games. They thought I was the one selling pot to the guys and it was going to get us all in trouble. Their job was to keep the Princes from getting in trouble with the police and the newspapers."

So, Wentworth admitted he sent his plainclothes agents to my apartment to entrap me into selling some pot. They looked like cops and I didn't fall for it. Then he had my place searched while I was out. They couldn't find anything."

Just recently, Wentworth had his guys follow me around again. I kept seeing the same car, wherever I went. Then, the night of the Lou Reed concert, while I was here with you, they searched my apartment again. They didn't find anything. So he is suspicious but he figures I am clean enough to work for SY. So he pulled me into his limo."

"Bridge, just so you know, I smoked a lot of pot when I was in school. But I quit cold turkey just before I graduated, and never used since then. I pass all of the drug tests at work. But I still hang out with the guys and they still have weed. So there are probably old photos of me smoking pot and maybe a new photo of someone trying to pass me a joint. So it looks like I'm still a pot head. That's what I think Wentworth is holding over me."

"OK, you were a stoner," said Bridgette with a little smile. "So, what happens next?"

"Well, Wentworth is going to pick me up next Saturday morning at the same place on Wilshire, hopefully no plainclothes cops this time."

Bridgette was thinking about all this new information. It all was adding up, but why hadn't she seen it before. Her interrogation was successful. She would have never imagined that Cliff could be involved in something this dangerous. But now, time to salvage the evening...

She wiggled right up next to him and stroked his arm. "You know you are crazy to do this. You are also very brave. I don't think you understand yet."

He visibly relaxed at her touch and turned toward her. He dropped his head and they began to kiss. Eventually they were lying together, embracing on the sofa.

"Jonesy...? You know, you being a secret agent is kind of a turn on...I might need to get something else off my chest."

"This time, does it have anything to do with the tube top?"

"Mmm-Hmmm!"

Twenty-four

After some morning tussling, SA Bridgette Evans was finally able to get Cliff showered, dressed, full of coffee and out the door, not before giving him some specific instructions.

"When you meet with Charles Wentworth next Saturday, don't tell him that you have spoken with me. The State Department may be so low on resources that they have to use you like this, but the FBI has plenty of resources.

"How can you protect me?" asked Cliff.

"Well, you are now my Confidential Informant. I own you! I can get you out of jail. I can send the cavalry." she smiled.

"Your instructions are to report back to me next Saturday at 6:00 PM sharp."

Then she smiled at him and said, "Bring a bottle of Pinot Noir this time."

Special Agent Evans went right in to her office, even though it was Memorial Day. She would have loved to spend the day with Cliff, brunching and strolling along the beach. He had tried to persuade her. And he was very persuasive, she smiled to herself.

But this was more important. Her assignment was to uncover illegal foreign agents here in the US, and especially on the west coast, with all of the technology businesses there. She had been mostly looking for Russian agents. The Russians had been playing the spy game for decades and were very good at it. Most of them spoke excellent English and were very hard to pin down.

Then relations were established with China at the beginning of the year, and China started pushing agents into the US. Again, it was very hard to distinguish their spies because they were posing as students and business people. And our government was encouraging them to come here as students and businessmen.

But now, the Iranians were going to attempt to infiltrate hit squads into the county to get the royals and any other Iranian nationals that they didn't like. There were about fifty thousand Iranians in the US. Most of them were students and most of them were in southern California. So naturally, Iran would send its agents to southern California. They were probably fairly well trained. She knew to never underestimate an enemy! But they certainly weren't going to be as well trained as the Russians or Chinese. So they would make mistakes. And they would be visible if they were actively following targets.

And now she knew their targets. Cliff would be the go between for the FBI as well as SY. The FBI would shadow his Persian friends and be real protection in case they were targeted. And they would also keep that big, brave, dumshit Cliff from getting his ass shot off. It was a nice ass and she would miss it if anything bad happened to him. But maybe he wasn't as dumb as she thought. She couldn't stop thinking about him picking up those eleven trackers during counter-surveillance training. Eyes in the back of his head. And what about that drug dealer thing?

If they could apprehend and interrogate any Iranian agents, they could figure out which border crossings were compromised. And the bad guys must need help with documents like passports and drivers licenses after they got inside the US. She could get the counterfeiters too. So, her plan was to get inside the Iranian network and use their agents to roll up the Russian and Chinese agents.

If she could pull this off, Bridgette knew it would complete her current assignment and get her a nice promotion. It would probably involve a reassignment, hopefully to DC. That's where the action was. A woman had to work twice as hard as a man to get ahead in the FBI, but she was ambitious and was going to do it.

Twenty-five

Saturday, June 2nd arrived and Cliff Jones awoke to his alarm at 7:00AM. This was not his normal Saturday routine, but he wanted to comply with Charles Wentworth's instructions. If he did everything he was asked, Wentworth would certainly have to keep up his end of the deal, and destroy whatever it was that he was holding over Cliff. At 8:00 AM, he was strolling along the south side of Wilshire approaching Fairfax. No Member's Only jackets in sight. A black limousine slid through the intersection and came to a halt at the sidewalk. The right rear door opened, and Cliff climbed in.

Twenty-six

"Good morning Cliff!", called Charles Wentworth. "How are you this fine morning?"

Cliff wasn't really interested in small talk with this man; he just wanted to find out what he had to say and get on with it. "Okay, I guess. So, what is this meeting about?"

"Well", said Charles, "I received very good reports about you from Fred Alen. He says that you're a natural, and wants the FBI to recruit you."

"You might be in the way of that," Cliff commented flatly.

Charles chuckled, "Indeed I might! Or not, depending on how things go. So, let's get down to business."

"First, the most important thing you are going to do for us is to maintain an open line of communication between us and your friends. All of that dead drop, live drop stuff is for the 1940's spy novels. We are going to use the telephone as our primary link. The enemy is not in any position to tap phone lines here inside the United States. So it is safe to assume they are secure. Pay phones are ideal, especially if you verify that you are not being watched or listened to, and if you don't always use the same phone. If you check for microphones inside your home phone hand set on a regular basis, your home phone should be secure. Play some background music while using the phone and this should prevent anyone from listening to microphones planted in your apartment. Plus, we will sweep your apartment for listening devices every now and then."

"Great," muttered Cliff. "I guess they know their way around my apartment now."

Charles replied, "We don't expect any Iranian agents to be as sophisticated as the Russians, but it doesn't hurt to be prepared."

Charles reached in his pocket and pulled out a small plastic box. "Have you seen a pager before?"

Cliff smirked. "Spock just did a TV commercial for some beeper company, so yeah. I wouldn't know this for sure, but rumor on the street says that drug dealers love these."

Charles grimaced at that, then handed the device to Cliff. "We will page you if we need to talk. You have no reason to carry a pager at work, so it would arouse suspicions. Hide this in your apartment and check it every night when you get home. If you have a new message, it will have your contact phone number. Check your phone and play some background sound, music or a TV show, and call. The number connects you to our SY call center. When the operator answers, just say 'tallboy' and you will be connected. You might be connected to me if I am available, or one of my agents will read you a message."

"Cliff, if you need to reach me, you call the center and say 'tallboy return'. If I am available, you will be connected to me. If not, one of my agents will take your message. Any questions?"

"Nah. Pretty straightforward," said Cliff.

"OK then, you understand why you had the class in drops and communications. We can't communicate swiftly with this system, but at least our communications will be secure. If the enemy has access to our communications, the battle is basically over."

"Fred was really impressed with your success in his surveillance and counter-surveillance class. This is what will save you and your friends if trouble does come to town. To protect yourself, you will need to verify that our Persian friends are not under surveillance before you meet up with them. If you are seen with them, you will be in just as much danger as them."

"If you do discover that your friends are under surveillance, you are going to have the tricky job of figuring out who they are and what they are up to; at the same time not getting caught yourself. And it won't be my men following your friends any more. I have to remove the protective detail right after their graduation this Thursday."

"We have several concerns about who may be watching them in the future. The most likely and least worrisome is that some Iranians, probably students, already in country and sympathetic to Khoumaini might be asked to follow them around. That's not good because it will mean that the Princes' covers are blown. But those would be amateurs, easy to spot and certainly not killers. The big problem would be if trained agents slipped into the US from Iran and went after the family. They will probably go for the Shah's mother and sister first, and then the Princes. They wouldn't attempt to assassinate them right away; they would track your friends to determine their patterns and then plan an attack that they could do quickly and then get away."

"What do you think, Cliff?"

Cliff frowned. "I think I get it. No news is good news. We will only contact each other if something changes. So I get the classes in surveillance and communication. But why did you have me take the firearms class?"

Charles sighed. "I'm not really sure. I didn't think you would need it. I hope you won't need it. But you never handled a gun before. And now you have. You have some knowledge that could click in if you need it. That's it, I guess."

As the limo slowed down, Charles said, "And that's it for you! Good luck out there, young man!"

The door opened and Cliff stepped out.

Twenty-seven

Saturday afternoon, June 2nd, Special Agent Bridgette Evans was working in her apartment, sprucing up and preparing dinner for this evening. She was also working in her head, running through ideas and scenarios. Her current assignment with the FBI was to uncover enemy agents hiding or operating inside the States, especially the southwest; hence her posting to Los Angeles almost two years ago. She was working hardest on how these agents got into the country in the first place.

Bridgette had a strong suspicion that the Russians were entering from Mexico, using one identity, and then getting a new identity once they were in. She also suspected that any Iranian agents trying to get into the southwest would do the same. Getting a new identity once in the States would require a source located here. A place that would provide passports, driver's licenses and even firearms. Find this source and the FBI could roll it up in both directions, catching those already here and stopping new entries.

The Russians were very good at their game; they had been doing it for decades. But the Iranians were new to the game of running agents in a foreign country, especially one as far away as the US. They should be a lot easier to detect, especially since we know that their specific mission will be to kill the Shah and his family members. And now that she knew of Cliff Jones' connection to that royal family, she hoped to have a window into what was happening there.

This would be interesting, she thought. Agents didn't have romantic relationships with their confidential informants. But this was different, she rationalized. Their romantic relationship had developed before she recruited him as a CI. And though she knew it couldn't last forever, it was going quite nicely, very nicely, and Bridgette didn't want to stop. A girl deserves a little fun! She thought he would be just a boy toy, but then realized he had a lot more going on than that. He was both fun and interesting to be with, more experienced in love and life than you would expect from a twenty-four year old. And full of secrets, she had intuited correctly. Her natural curiosity, which made her an effective FBI investigator, cracked open a few of those secrets. His relationship with the Office of Security over at the State Department was the blockbuster of secrets. And he had just fallen into her lap, with a little push.

She drifted into her bedroom, and selected a V-neck top and matching mini skirt. She wrapped the skirt and tied it on her hip so it would open with each step. Then she tied the top just beneath her breasts and slipped into some Candies clogs. She added a tiny dab of perfume behind each earlobe. That would keep his attention from wandering!

At 6:00 PM, there was a knock on the door. Bridgette smiled: punctual, too. She opened the door and saw Cliff Jones standing there, with a bottle of wine in one hand and a single red rose in the other, and a very distracted look on his face. She took his arm and drew him in, closed the door, placed the wine and flower on the entrance table, guided his hands to her bare hips, slid her arms up and around his neck, pressed her body to his and gave him a just a bit too long kiss on the lips. She noticed his color darken as she disengaged. He took a ragged breath. Nothing like unsettling your witness before the interrogation, she thought.

"Jonesy, so glad you could make it. I know you have such a busy schedule now that you are a spy as well as a banker!" she teased. "And the rose, how romantic!" She placed the bottle of wine on the kitchen counter, next to two glasses and a bottle opener. "Would you mind opening the wine and pouring us a drop?"

He hesitated as he finally took his eyes off her for a second, coughed "Sure," then walked into the kitchen. As he worked on the bottle Bridgette idly rubbed the rose across her chest and could see his eyes darting from the wine bottle to her. "Such a lovely flower, don't you think?" she asked.

After they clinked glasses and sipped, Bridgette said "Nice choice of Pinot Noir. Is wine tasting another of your hidden talents?

That finally broke the ice. Cliff laughed and said, "Another confession for you, Special Agent Evans. I have a friend who works the wine section at Trader Joe's. Hasn't steered me wrong yet."

Bridgette smiled, "Well, lets sit down and chat. Business before pleasure. How was your meeting with Wentworth from the State Department?"

Cliff sighed. "Not very pleasurable. Wentworth said that Fred Alen wants to recruit me to the FBI. We know why that can't happen. The bastard has me by the balls and wanted to rub it in."

"Did he give you any instructions or directives?" asked Bridgette.

"Well, he gave me this," handing the beeper from his pocket to Bridgette.

She regarded it, and took note of the phone number on its label.

"I'm supposed to hide this somewhere in my apartment, and check it every night when I get home. If there is a message I ring their call center. I can call from home if it is safe; otherwise I have to use a pay phone. I give a code word to the operator and then someone gives me the message."

"If I need to reach him, I call the same number and give the code words to the operator. Then I will be connected to him or someone who can take my message. That is pretty much the whole communication plan."

"What about your Persian friends, the royalty?" Bridgette asked.

"OK, State Department has to stop watching us this week, right after their graduation this Thursday. So, no more protection."

"Any time I get together with them, Wentworth wants me to survey the area first. Make sure no one is watching me, then check if anyone is watching them. There shouldn't be any trouble for a few weeks, but if I do see any suspicious people, he wants me to try and follow them, get their information, then report to him."

"Follow them? Holy shit Cliff! What is he thinking?" cried Bridgette. "And, is there anything else?

"Not really," Cliff answered. "I understand why the communications and surveillance training. But I asked Wentworth why the firearms class and he gave some half-baked answer."

"Yeah, because he knows you could get filled with lead, Cliff!" she said. "I'm really pissed off at how this Wentworth wants you to do surveillance on trained killers when you have no experience at all."

Bridgette stood up, walked to her telephone and dialed the number on the beeper. Cliff could hear a click as it connected and then a double tone. At that tone, Bridgette punched in a series of numbers on her keypad and then hung up. She handed the beeper to Cliff and said with a smile, "The game is on!"

In response to his puzzled look, she said, "We're sharing your beeper with the State Department. Just don't tell them!" Just then, the beeper buzzed and vibrated. "Look at the number on the display," she said. "That is my office number. You call me when you see that message. If I don't answer, someone else will. You can trust them. Identify yourself and they will give you my message. If you need to contact me, identify yourself if I'm not there and they will take your message. When I am out in the field, we normally use radio cars. So I will get any message from you pretty quickly. Just business calls to the office number – no lovey dovey stuff, OK?"

"What is the point of all this?" asked Cliff.

"Cliff, you're working for me now! You are my Confidential Informant, my CI, my double agent. Unlike State, the FBI can protect you and your friends."

"You are going to share with me all of the communications between your friends and State. If you detect that you or your friends are being followed, you are NOT to track the followers. You call me immediately! The FBI will track them down and deal with them. That's what we do!"

Cliff was still puzzled. "But why are you getting involved in this?"

"Cliff, this is my assignment! It's the reason I am here in LA. I am trying to uncover foreign agents operating here in this country. And you and your friends are going to lead me right to them."

Cliff wasn't puzzled any more. "I get it now. We are your bait!" he exclaimed.

"I knew you would figure it out." she said. "And you would be okay working under me."

"It won't be the first time I've worked under you, and it always works out just fine.", he joked.

Bridgette shook his hand and said, "Welcome aboard! But now it's time for dinner. I made a chicken cordon bleu to go with your lovely pinot noir, so lets eat!"

And eat they did. And sip the wine. The dining table was now in candlelight. Cliff was impressed as before with Bridgette's gourmet cooking skills. They were chatting about all sorts of things: her cooking skills, his wine skills. It was the chatter of lovers. The new relationship added to their existing relationship became the chatter of co-workers: the excitement of hiding a romantic relationship at work. Back to the chatter of lovers. Bridgette saw the gleam in his eyes. Maybe it was the wine. She was feeling warm and light herself. It was not just the wine. He was standing behind her as she attempted to wash the dishes. His hands around her waist. Sliding up, cupping. Sliding down, stroking. Entering the slit in her skirt.

"Jonesy...I think its time for a little practice. You know...the part where you work under me...

Twenty-eight

Thursday afternoon, June 7th, Cliff Jones called his friend Cy from his desk at the Bank of America. "Hey Cy, congrats on you guys graduating today. Sorry I couldn't be there – I had to work today."

"Bullshit, you just didn't want to stand in the hot sun for hours like we did today! Kind of a pain in the ass, but we got our diplomas." replied Cy.

"So, you guys want to go out and celebrate? I can get you guys on Saturday afternoon if you want."

"Hey, man, that sounds good," said Cy, "But we will come and get you. No more tooling around town in that beater of yours. We'll go out in style, man!"

"Cool, you got your new car! Alright, what did you get?"

"Surprise, man! You'll find out Saturday. We'll be honking and making a whole lot of noise outside your apartment about 4 o'clock."

Twenty-nine

Sure enough, the honking began outside of Cliff's apartment about 4 o'clock on Saturday afternoon. Cliff was ready to go, so he was outside in no time. And there were Cy, Kammy and Goalie, standing around a brand new 1979 Oldsmobile Cutlass Supreme Brougham. It was red, with the matching red hubcaps, red leather interior and white vinyl top with T-tops. Cliff immediately yelled "Shotgun!" and jumped into the front passenger seat. The others poured in, with Cy at the wheel as usual. "Awesome car guys!" he shouted. "Looks fully loaded. What it got?

Kammy got into it. "Except for being an Oldsmobile, its got nothing in common with that '65 junker you were kidding us about. Its got the 350 V8, four speed trans, power steering, power brakes, disk brakes up front, power windows and locks, A/C and the 8-track stereo. This baby moves!"

"So Cliff, where do you wanna go?" asked Cy.

Cliff had already thought about this. "Its pretty warm and clear today. Let's take it up to Griffith, and you can show off on the curves up the hill." Cliff directed Cy east on Wilshire, then left on Vermont, then said, "Just stay on Vermont until we get to the top."

Cy had fun powering the car uphill and through the curves until they reached the top. Cliff said, "Why don't you take a slow lap past the observatory and then park on the edge at the back of the lot."

Cy parked, they all got out and stood looking over the edge, admiring the view of the entire L.A. basin spread out below them. An LAPD squad car circled the lot and stopped parallel to the Cutlass. The windows rolled down. The four of them turned and looked at the two officers in the car. "Was that your car we just heard on the hillside coming up here?"

Cliff stepped up, "Yes officers, this is my friend's new car. A graduation present. Its loaded. We just needed to see what it can do."

The cop at the passenger window gave a little smirk. "Now that you've checked it out, you can keep the noise down in the future. Nice car, by the way. Have a good afternoon, gentlemen." The squad car pulled away and headed back down the hill.

Once the cops were out of sight, they all laughed. "Thanks for handling the cops for me", said Cy.

Cliff spat, "Those fuckers! How many times have they pulled me over when I was driving Mabel. You guys were with me once, remember? It's all "license and registration" and "step out of the car". Then when they realize we're not Mexicans, its all "drive carefully, sir, have a good night, sir." Driving While Brown, D.W.B. Its bullshit! Now here we are in broad daylight, white guys, nice clothes, new car, probably deserved a ticket for exhibition of speed, and they just slow down so they can check out your car."

They are still laughing. Cy said, "See Cliff, you should have dumped that junker for something better long ago. Then you'd get some respect."

Thirty

Cliff called out, "Hey guys, there's another reason I brought you up here besides the view. I've got something private to tell you, and nobody can eavesdrop on us up here." He said to them, "I recently found out that our US State Department has been keeping an eye on you guys ever since you came here for University. Did you know that?"

Cy said, "When we first got here, some guys gave us the idea that they would be watching us, to make sure we didn't get in trouble. We thought Shah was behind it because he didn't want any more embarrassments like our idiot cousin up in northern California. You know, the one who attacked a cop and went to jail. Every now and then we see some guys watching us, but never any problem."

"We know that the State Department is protecting Auntie Shams and the queen mom. They were up there during the riot in Beverly Hills, and they got the ladies out of there in a hurry, drove them straight out to the safe house in Palm Springs. But they didn't offer us any help. That's why we called you to get us."

Cliff said, "So now that the Shah is out of power, the State Department has to stop protecting his family. So no one will be watching you guys anymore."

Cy was puzzled. "How do you know about all of this?"

Cliff told them, "Those guys you have been seeing are agents from the State Department, and they were watching you and me. They were the plainclothes cops who tried to catch me selling pot. I found out that they broke in and searched my place. So a few weeks ago they kidnapped me so their boss could talk to me. He must have pictures of us partying together because he is blackmailing me to work for him. He told me I will lose my job if I don't help him. So he wants me to report on you guys. They are very interested in what you are going to do next. Since the U.S. Government has to try to kiss up to Khoumaini, they can't be seen helping or even talking with the opposition. But behind the scenes, they know Khoumaini is a problem and want to help anyone who could get rid of him. Like you and your family."

"So what are you going to do, Cliff?", asked Cy.

"Hell, I'm with you guys! I want to help you however I can. And I'll tell that guy whatever you want me to tell him. But he doesn't need to know everything. He says he wants to help, but I don't see how he can offer any protection, and you might be needing it."

"What does that mean, we might be needing protection?" asked Kam.

"I hate to say," said Cliff, "but there are rumors that Khoumaini is sending out death squads to kill the Shah and his family. You guys."

"We didn't saying anything to you, but the family has been aware of this for a while. We are talking about what to do. And it is still secret, but Shah is traveling to Mexico City tomorrow. It will be easier for us to see him, and safer there. We guys can move around pretty easily in Mexico. Who will notice three more tanned faces!", Cy said with a smile. "So, what's the deal? What are you going to do?"

"So here is what I can do. Some time soon, people might start watching you. They won't be the good guys, but they won't be the killers either. At first.", Cliff said. "So we will all keep our eyes open. And if we can get some info, like a license plate from a car following you, we can get some real help. Not from the State Department but from some people who have real muscle. So I have some tips to share with you, to know if you are being followed, and what to do next."

"All right," said Cy, "I'm hungry and thirsty. Enough of this secret agent stuff for now."

Thirty-one

Back in the new Cutlass, Cliff directed Cy down the hill, left on Los Feliz, and followed the merge onto Western. "Just cruise down Western to 11th Street and grab a parking spot at El Cholo's. It's the classic USC celebration spot."

Sure enough, the place was packed with USC grad parties. They were lucky to get a booth in the corner. Carmen came over to take their orders. They started with pitchers of margaritas, chips, salsa and guac, which got the party going, then ordered from the famous combination meals. Cliff asked the graduates what they wanted to do, now that school was over for them.

Cy was a little philosophical, "You know, we would be going home right now like we used to, but that can't happen. And, can you believe, Thursday there were people everywhere on campus for graduation, but Friday morning, it was crickets? Everybody was gone. Its a ghost town. We talked about spending the summer there, but there's nothing going on."

Cliff laughed, "I warned you what it was like. I spent a bunch of summers down there, bored shitless. That's why I moved as soon as I got that first promotion. You should get out of there."

Cy said, 'Yeah, we started talking about that yesterday, after we saw how quiet it was. It would be safer and more fun to be in a crowded area. What about your neighborhood, Cliff?"

Cliff said, "Where I live is nice, but its a bedroom community. Just boring working folks like me. After work, I sit in the pub watching baseball with a bunch of old guys. You want to go to where the fun is: the beach!"

"So, what do you suggest, Cliff?"

Cliff said, "If I were you guys, I would get in that shiny new car, get on the Santa Monica Freeway all the way to the end, and then drive up and down the coast, checking out all the beach towns. Start with Santa Monica and Venice, they're pretty funky. Then check out the Marina. Its really swanky there. Lots of stuff happening. You guys would fit right in. If you want, go south of the airport. Manhattan, Hermosa and Redondo beaches are cool. Pretty laid back. You could learn to surf and play beach volleyball."

Thirty-two

Cliff Jones had a few quiet weeks in the middle of June. Bridgette was too busy with her assignment to take a day, or even a night off. Cliff was aware that even if they blurted the "love" word to each other, there was never going to be a real relationship. Bridgette was already in a commitment, to her job with the FBI. Despite this knowledge, Cliff persevered. He knew he would never get this close to someone like her again. He was in love with her. He would tell her, too. Her independence and self confidence, her wit and sense of humor, intelligence and absolutely mesmerizing sexuality had him completely captivated. On the occasions when they did get together, they got along so well that the various surprises that they sprung on each other barely caused a bump in their mutual desire. It seemed she could just turn off her job and immerse herself in their relationship. Or maybe was he just her boy toy, an occasional break from her job? Oh well, who cares? he thought. It won't last forever, so enjoy it while he can. When it's over it will hurt for a while, then eventually there will be someone else. Right?

Cliff's Persian friends were silent, too. Calls to their apartment were unanswered. They had to be making plans, both to move away from downtown, and also what to do about their situation. The rumors he had shared had become real. The newspapers were plastered with stories about the Iranian "Death Squad" that Khoumaini had sent after the Shah. It was revealed that this squad had already reached the Bahamas, which explained the Shah's quick escape to Mexico City earlier in the month. Were they going to try to track down the entire family and kill them all? It seemed far away. This is the United States, not the Bahamas, not Mexico. It can't happen here, can it?

Gas continued to be a problem in Los Angeles. Cliff was taking the Wilshire Boulevard number 20 bus to and from work, so he had no problem there. It was only a few minutes slower than driving himself. But not having enough gasoline constrained the activities he could do. Walking around the corner to Tom Bergin's Pub provided a decent meal, cold beer, the Dodgers on TV and fellow fans to talk with. He didn't want to make this a habit, though. There were too many guys he recognized every time he visited. He wasn't going to become a barfly. So he took Mabel to work on the appropriate odd-even day and got in a gas line. After a couple of hours reading a paperback and rolling his car along, he was able to get a full tank just before dark. Now he could have a little fun on the weekend.

That night, the light on his beeper was flashing for the first time. It was the State Department number that he called, went through the code word rigmarole, and had a brief message read to him: "Please report." He went through his callback procedure, didn't get Charles Wentworth, who was probably at home with pipe and slippers, thought Cliff, then left a return message: "Nothing to report." They were probably just testing him to make sure he knew the procedure.

Cliff longed to call the other number in the beeper, and catch Bridgette at her FBI desk, but he stayed within their agreement, which he called the separation between church and state, and didn't contact her at work with personal calls. He did call her home phone. No answer as usual. At work, her Confidential Informant, and at home her boy toy, thought Cliff.

Thirty-three

On Saturday, June 30th, Cliff followed his usual routine. Dressed for the courts, he headed to the Farmers Market for a coffee and light breakfast before basketball. He was unconsciously looking all around at the corner of Wilshire and Fairfax, but no Members Only jackets and no black limo in sight. A slight shiver at the thought, though. And an anticipatory peek into the market, remembering when he first bumped into Bridgette. Again, a shiver at the memory and then a strange thought: who bumped into who? But she wasn't there and he continued his stroll to the basketball courts in Pan Pacific park.

Cliff played in multiple games of three-on-three, forming and re-forming teams to play "winners" as players came and went. The smog was better than it had been for the last three days, but the temperature was well into the eighty's by noon. A bunch of the players decided to call it a morning and walked over for nooners at El Coyote. Cliff had tacos and some beers with everyone, then wandered home. There was nothing like a Saturday afternoon nap to refresh after basketball and beers, and after that a shave and shower before hitting the town. His phone was ringing as he was drying off and he scooted out of the bathroom to answer it.

"Cliff!", calls Cy. "Check this out. You told us to keep an eye open for someone following us?"

Cliff felt a sudden jolt of adrenaline.

"So, we've been driving around the beaches, looking for a place to rent. We keep seeing this car behind us. We thought we saw them on Flower, then on the Santa Monica freeway and now, down here. Like you said, don't let them know we see them. So I can't get a license or anything like that. But there are two guys in it, could be Persians like us. And I think its a Torino. blue like your car but better, you know, not all faded out."

Cliff asked, "So, where are you now?"

"We're in Manhattan Beach. We're circling around. We're gonna park and go into Panchos for late lunch. You know where that is?"

Cliff says, "Yeah, corner of Rosecrans. So, park on that roof lot on Highland and stay in the restaurant like forty-five minutes, then leave. Turn right out of the parking lot and drive around a little bit, then head home. When you get home, just go up into the apartment and act normal. I'm gonna follow them to your place, and when they see you tucked in, maybe they'll go home. I'm gonna try to follow them home and get their address. So don't look for me and just ignore those guys. I will call you when its all over."

Thirty-four

On the drive down to Manhattan Beach, Cliff Jones had time to think about what he was doing. First, he'd screwed up his weekend drive. His tank was full, but a drive to Manhattan, then to downtown, then following these turkeys was going to use up a bunch of his gas. Then, what about Bridgette telling him not to follow anyone. He smiled to himself: It's easier to ask forgiveness than permission. And what was she going to do to him? Spank him? Handcuff him? Fun!

Like they had all discussed, the first people to follow the princes would not likely be the pros. Someone saw some Persians in a brand new car and got curious. It's probably some Persian students trying to figure out how another Persian would have enough money to buy a new car. Or, if that Iranian student group was getting more organized, someone is trying to get locations of the Persians here in the US. Then, if he follows them home, where will that be? He hoped it wouldn't be Northridge. Cal State up there had much lower tuition than USC or UCLA, so it was popular for the less affluent Iranian students. And that's where they had that convention of Iranian students right after the riot. He remembered the photo showing the hammer and sickle on the wall next to the podium. But Cliff had only been that far north in the valley once or twice, so he didn't know the streets as well as the lower valley or the basin. Or if he was lucky, they would live near UCLA. Plenty of commie and Khoumaini lovers at that school. Bruins!

Cliff drove Fairfax south until it merged with La Cienega, then continued south until La Cienega put him on the 405 south at Manchester. He exited at Rosecrans and drove west. He was asking himself how two amateur sleuths would stake out a parked car in the parking lot. If they parked in the lot, they risked being seen and unless they went in the restaurant, someone might ask what they are doing there. But outside the lot, they have no idea which way the Cutlass will exit. If it were him, he would park on Rosecrans just below the restaurant. As long as the car wasn't right in front of the entrance, no one would notice a guy sitting in a car. And the other guy would wait on the corner of Rosecrans and Highland. He would keep moving around, crossing the street, smoking a cigarette, but always in sight of the parking lot exit. As soon as the Cutlass exits the lot, the other guy would be only half a block from the car. He waves, and the driver picks him up. Then they resume following the Cutlass.

So Cliff took Rosecrans to Alma Avenue and turned left. Then he turned right on 36th Street, and right again onto Manhattan Avenue. He stopped just before Rosecrans, and noticing the carports were all empty at the corner house, backed Mabel into the center port. He hoped this would just take a minute. He hopped out of his car and peeked around the corner and up Rosecrans. What luck! One block up, parked on the corner of Bayview, was a blue Torino. He walked that block briskly, noted the license plate number, saw a head in the driver's seat, and quickly continued into Bayview, then around the block back to his car.

Once he was back in Mabel, he parked her in the street at the stop sign, leaving enough room that cars could get around him. Then he turned off the motor and lifted the hood. Nobody wants to get involved with a young guy and a broken down car. Most traffic just sped up a bit to get by. If anyone slowed down to take a look, Cliff would lean in under the hood, reach in, then shake his head. That got rid of them. A cop even drove by and purposely looked away. Mabel, his secret weapon, made him the invisible man.

After a few minutes, Cliff heard an automobile engine start up. A quick peek around the corner showed the Torino starting to pull away from the curve. No rush. He knew what Cy would do. Once the Torino turned right onto Highland, Cliff closed the hood and started his car. He turned right and drove east on Rosecrans. As he approached the 405 Freeway he saw a gas line at a station just before the northbound on ramp and joined it, leaving a few feet in front of him for an easy exit. Almost immediately another car lined up behind him and got really close. Good, because that hid his license plate from view. Some busybody might see that he was lining up on the wrong day and make a scene.

Cliff knew that Cy was not familiar with the South Bay, so he would head south on Highland as directed, but would double back toward Rosecrans after a few stop lights, then head east to the 405. Sure enough, about five minutes later, Cliff saw a red Cutlass approaching in his side view mirror. Three cars later it was followed by a blue Torino. So far, so good. He waited for six cars to pass before jumping out of the line. As the three car convoy entered the freeway and headed north, Cliff stayed a good half mile back. Cliff was pretty sure that Cy would stick to the freeway route, so he jumped off the 405 at Manchester and headed east toward the Harbor Freeway. Manchester was usually a total mess during the work week, but was pretty quiet on the weekends. That saved a lot of time. He reached the Harbor Freeway without delay, headed north and exited at 37th Street. Two quick lefts put him on Flower Street, where he quickly turned right onto 37th Place behind the Trojan Barrel and parked facing west. The only time the Torino had an opportunity to see him was in the gas line on Rosecrans, so he probably hadn't been seen. However, he would take no chances. He already had the most important information – the license plate number.

Fifteen minutes later, Cliff saw the red Cutlass glide by in his rear view mirror. Cy would turn left into the parking lot behind their apartment complex. Then the blue Torino glided by. He gave it a minute, then got out and peeked around the corner. Sure enough, the Torino had continued past the parking lot driveway to confirm they were in there, then parked on the corner next to the Barrel. Cliff saw one of the living room windows open in the apartment, and heard music come out. Nothing happened for a few minutes. Then, the Torino's passenger door opened, and the passenger climbed out. He started to walk toward Cliff. Cliff ran to his car, got in and ducked down. His heart was racing. Had he been seen? Did they know they had been followed? How could that be possible?

Cliff ventured a quick pop-up peek out the window and dropped back down. It took a couple of seconds to process what he had seen, but then he almost broke out laughing. The passenger had his back toward Cliff and was peeing on the wall of the restaurant. Another peek a moment later showed the guy walking quickly back to the Torino. A minute later, the driver came around the corner and also relieved himself. You couldn't do that in broad daylight during the school year, but it was so quiet during the summer break that Cliff was the only witness.

Cliff waited a few minutes for them to get back in their car. If he was right, the followers had been driving all day without a break opportunity. They didn't know the area very well or they would have ducked into Julie's Trojan Barrel to use the restroom. No one would have challenged them. And after driving all day, their gas was probably low, so they couldn't follow the Cutlass again if it took off on another drive. So they would return home and report.

Cliff would have to be careful since the followers might have noticed his car during their pee break. He watched from the corner as they started their car and made the hard right to get on northbound Figueroa. Back in his car he saw them slide past his spot on 37th Place. He didn't turn out onto Figueroa until they were completely out of sight on 37th Street, heading to the freeway. He turned very slowly onto 37th Street and was rewarded with the sight of a blue car turning left on Hope, which was toward the northbound entrance. At this point Cliff gambled that they would go west on the Santa Monica freeway, which seemed to him the fastest way to either UCLA or Cal State Northridge. Which meant he purposely lost them, intending to traverse the Harbor to Santa Monica interchange out of their sight. Once through the interchange and heading west on the Santa Monica, he sped up and saw a blue Torino in the distance, glad for that distinctive rear end on the Ford. He dropped back again, intending to get on the northbound 405 well behind them. Once on the 405, he moved up until he spotted the Torino, then dropped back a few cars and got into the right lane. Their two cars were out of sight of each other, but Cliff would immediately see if the Torino used an off-ramp.

Cliff really didn't want to go to Northridge to follow these guys since he didn't know the area that well. The valley is pretty much a grid, but if you don't know the streets, you could get in trouble. Cliff remembered turning into that dead end with Fred Alen that Saturday in May. Not good. He knew the west side much better even though the streets weaved a bit as you got into the hilly areas. And as hoped, he saw a blue car getting ready to exit at Wilshire. Wilshire was pretty crowded, so Cliff could get much closer without attracting attention, but when the Torino turned north on Veteran, there was a problem. Veteran is a long, slow, straight residential street with a cemetery on one side. Once he turned on Veteran, Cliff immediately pulled to the curb. He knew that those guys could see all the way back to Wilshire in their rear view. So he waited until they were completely out of sight, then drove ahead one block. Catching a glimpse of the blue tail end, he pulled to the curb again. He did this several nerve-wracking times until he completely lost them. Afraid he had lost them for good he sped up and blew through the Strathmore intersection, luckily spotting a flash of blue already around the corner and halfway up the hill on Strathmore.

Cliff had been on pins and needles, knowing they were close to home. As he made a mid-street U-turn and got himself going up Strathmore he felt a little more confident. He drove until he crested each hill and he could see the Torino in front of him. Since they were already at the bottom of the next hill, they could not see behind to his hilltop in their mirrors. So Cliff could see them but they couldn't see him. He followed for several blocks until they turned left, and up a hill on Landfair. He waited until they were out of sight and then turned left himself. He could see them approaching the top of the hill, and if they looked in their mirrors they could see him. But if Cliff pulled over, he would lose them. So he continued slowly and deliberately up the hill and saw them turn right into the driveway of an underground garage. He drove by, then grabbed a parking spot in front of the next building and shut off the motor.

Cliff had done it! He had run the fox to ground! But something had been nagging him for the last hour. He needed just a little more information to complete this task. Cliff got out and crossed the street, then walked slowly past the building where the Torino had parked. He noted the street number of the nine story building, 504 Landfair, then peered across the street and into the building's lobby, one level up from the garage entrance. It was quiet for a moment, then he could see activity, figures moving around. They moved off to one side, then it was quiet. After several minutes, a window opened near the top floor. OK, they are in their apartment. Cliff was about to walk down into the garage when he thought better of it. What if someone caught him down there? He didn't belong down there. Instead he got back into Mabel, and drove around the block. When he got back to the driveway, he slowly drove in. Eyes adjusting to the darker garage, he found the blue Torino and parked next to it. He got out and did a quick look around, this time noting the expiration date on the rear license plate and the permit number on the window sticker. Otherwise, it was a plain-Jane Torino, no other distinguishing features. He climbed into Mabel and got moving quickly. As he was about to drive up the ramp, someone appeared in the garage. Cliff waved at them, hand in front of his face as he got out of there, hoping their eyes were adjusting to the dark and couldn't see him. He left. Not too fast, but fast. Right turn on Landfair, then a quick right on Gayley, which took him all the way back down to Wilshire. A left turn on Wilshire got him headed home, now driving on autopilot on his home turf.

As Cliff calmed down from his adrenaline high, he started to review all that had happened. Some of it was a little scary, but it was all pretty exciting. Had he messed up? Forgotten anything he should have noticed? What would he report? What would he not share? Without question, he would call Bridgette first. Give her a head start. Would she be pissed at him for following them, against her direct orders? Let her decide how long he should wait before telling Wentworth. But he would call Wentworth eventually. It was part of his deal.

When Cliff finally arrived home on Alandele and shut down Mabel, he sorrowfully noted how close the gas gauge was to "empty". So much for his weekend plans.

Thirty-five

Upstairs in his apartment, Cliff Jones reviewed in his mind what he would tell Bridgette. No sense putting it off, he dialed her office number. He hoped she would answer herself. If would prove that she really was spending all those hours working if he found her at her desk late on a Saturday afternoon.

After three rings, the call was picked up. "This is Special Agent Evans. Who is calling, please?" came a crisp, professional, no-nonsense voice.

"Bridgette, it's Cliff Jones," he replied. "I have some information for you."

"Really!", she said. "Let me grab a pen...there! Okay, tell me what you've got."

"Okay Bridgette, around three today I got a call from my Persian friends. They were being followed. So I drove out and got the information about their followers. There were two men, possibly Persians, driving a mid '70s blue Ford Torino." He then recited the license plate number and the expiration date, and then the Parking Permit number and the home address where they parked and went in.

The phone was quiet for a minute. Cliff thought he heard a tapping sound in the background, like a pen rapping on a desk. He imagined the look on Bridgette's face. "So Cliff, how exactly did you come to get all of this information about these guys, especially their address?" She didn't sound pleased.

Cliff: "...umm...I guess I followed them home..."

In a flat voice, Bridgette said, "I thought so...tell me where you followed them."

So Cliff filled her in on the details, from driving down to

Manhattan Beach and picking up the license plate number, then getting downtown ahead of the others with his alternate route, and finally following the Torino to Westwood and its final stop. He mentioned driving into the garage for cover where he got the expiration date and permit number.

"You DO know what you did wrong, don't you?", she asked very firmly.

"Yes," he said quietly.

"Anyway, this information is actionable. We can deal with the other issue later.", she said. "Have you passed this information to the State Department yet?

Cliff answered, "No, but I will need to give this to them soon."

"I understand," she said. "But wait until tomorrow evening to inform them."

She asked, "You're calling from your apartment, aren't you? Will you be home later? Are you going out or anything?"

"Well, I was going out.", he said sadly. "But now my car is on empty. I can't go anywhere until I get some gas. So I'll just be sitting here...at home...all alone..."

He thought he might have heard a giggle. But then an all-business voice said, "OK Cliff, I am going to call you later. It will probably be pretty late, once I finish processing your information. But I will definitely call you, so stay awake and answer the phone."

Thirty-six

SA Bridgette Evans sat at her desk, sighed, and shook her head. She should have known something like this would happen. Cliff was impulsive and wanted to get the information. But if he had been seen, and if those were real bad guys, he would be dead in that downtown alley.

But he did the surveillance properly, to the book. And didn't get caught. And the followers didn't act like bad guys. And he did get very good information. Remembering to check the license expiration date was genius. Since it was expired, it gave any law enforcement agency probable cause to pull over that car. And crossing the registration with a roster from that apartment tower would give names and probably immigration status of at least one of them. And she would squeeze him and he would sing like a canary.

So Bridgette submitted each piece of information to the appropriate agencies. And knew they didn't work as hard as her. So it would be late Monday morning before she received any information in return.

What to do with Cliff? She had rationalized that their personal relationship had come first, so she could keep it going even after bringing him in as a CI. But he hadn't followed instructions. And she couldn't bring him into the office. The men were clueless, but the other ladies in the office would take one look at her and Cliff, and they would know. Perhaps she was being over-protective of him, because of their relationship. She wouldn't hesitate to ask any other CI to try and get all the information they could.

She could just see him sitting in his apartment now, feeling excited about a successful first mission, but apprehensive because of her displeasure that he didn't follow orders. And that sob story about stuck at home, what a joke! Any other

Saturday he would be at Bergin's watching the Dodgers and drinking with his buddies. She decided that nothing more would get done in the office tonight, so she would go home and get ready. For her next mission. Which was Cliff. He had done well and deserved congratulations. And he had done wrong and deserved...discipline? Hmm, this would be fun!

Thirty-seven

Bridgette Evans left her office around eight o'clock that Saturday night. Cliff Jones' information was going to yield some good results, but not tonight. She got to her apartment in about twenty minutes. She freshened up and planned what to wear. For Cliff, her black leather miniskirt and strappy pumps. Always in fashion. She picked a filmy black sequined blouse and left it open about a button past trouble. His attention would be right there! When ready, she dialed over to his apartment and he answered right away. Good boy! He must be on pins and needles. "Cliff, I will pick you up in front of your apartment in ten minutes. Dress nice." she said quickly, then hung up. His head must be spinning. She planned to arrive a few minutes early, just to see what would happen.

Cliff Jones' head was indeed spinning. Dress fast! Designer jeans. Button down dress shirt, top two buttons open. Blue blazer. Oh, and stuff a tie in the pocket just in case. He was out the door, down the stairs and at the curb in eight minutes, just as a black S series BMW turned the corner. Really!? Bridgette? But it was her face in the driver's seat and her voice calling, 'Get In!".

Once he was in the car, Bridgette sped off. He was trying to pay attention to where they were going, and he thought it was Wilshire to La Cienega north, but he was really paying attention to the legs coming out of that miniskirt and the blouse that couldn't stay closed. Bridgette had seen his outfit as he got in, and said, "Not bad for dressing at the last minute. You'll want to put on that tie you brought."

"How did you know I have a tie? It's in my right pocket. You can't see that?"

"Of course I can't see it. But I knew you would be prepared. My Boy Scout!"

"Never was a boy scout," mumbled Cliff as he put on his tie. He was just straightening it when Bridgette pulled up to the valet station at Lawry's the Prime Rib. As the car doors were opened by valets, Cliff heard, "Welcome Ms. Evans! Nice to see you again." Cliff and Bridgette walked in the door where the maitre d' repeated the greeting and led them to a spacious booth in the back of the room. As they slid into the booth, he asked, "Martinis ma'am?" , saw the nod and responded, "Of course, thank you!"

Bridgette turned to Cliff, took his face in both hands, turned it to hers and kissed him on the lips, long and deep enough not to be chaste. "Good evening Jonesy!" she said, then asked, "So, what's up?"

Jones shook his head and said, "Fifteen minutes ago I was in my apartment listening to some jazz, then the phone rang... Nice car, by the way. I'm impressed. But you're hotter than that car. If we get any closer in this booth, you'll know what's up! And Lawry's! What's the special occasion? Did I forget your birthday?"

Bridgette laughed. "Lawry's is my go-to place. They have a late-night menu, and when I scurry in after work just before closing, they treat a single girl like a queen. But we are celebrating tonight! Here come the martinis!"

They raised glasses, sipped, and Bridgette called, "Here's to me! I landed a new CI! He is quirky and hard to control, but he got the job done. And here's to you, Cliff Jones, successfully completing your first mission! Not quite as planned, but successful none the less."

"So I'm sorry you burned all of your gas and your Saturday night plans were ruined. Hopefully I can make it up to you with a nice dinner. I know you like my cooking, but they do okay here."

A server brought a big salad bowl and went through the Lawry's spinning bowl routine, leaving them each with a plateful of salad.

"You know Cliff," said Bridgette, "I may have been a little bit overprotective when I ordered you not to follow anyone. I just didn't want you to get hurt."

Cliff replied, "I thought about that. Normally you wouldn't stop an informer from gathering the information you want, so why me? The SY has no problem with me following leads."

"Cliff, its because I like you too much. I have to confess that there are times when I have avoided you so we won't get too close in our relationship. I would really hate for you to fall in love with me and then have your heart broken when I am transferred out of here."

"A little late for that," Cliff said. Raising his head and looking into her eyes, he said, "I am already in love with you. I love you Bridgette. I have known it for a while. I just haven't said anything because I didn't want to spook you." He paused a moment.

"But please don't freak out. I thought about this a lot. I realize that we can't have a regular relationship. You have a commitment, and its not to me or any other person. You are dedicated to your career, and I understand you have to be that way to succeed. I am proud of you for how strong you are. So I am just asking that you share some time with me. Let's go on dates, go on weekenders, have fun! When you leave, I will be very sad. It will hurt for a long time. But I'll survive. And when I think of us, I'll know that we made the most of every minute."

"Oh Cliff!," she said. "Jonesy, I didn't expect this from you. I look at you and see a twenty-four year old kid. Then you tell me this. You just broke my heart! Now I have second thoughts about everything."

"No no!" cried Cliff. "It's all good! Don't be sad! Let's enjoy! Celebrate! Dry the tears and smile. By the way, I think they are bringing the meat!

Cliff and Bridgette enjoyed the rest of the show: presentation of the prime rib, then a shared sundae and coffees to finish. Afterward, it only took Bridgette a few minutes to drive into Cliff's neighborhood and pull into an empty parking spot.

"Are you going to invite me up?" she asked coyly.

"I don't want to keep you from your work", he cracked back.

"You're my work tonight, buckaroo. You disobeyed a direct order. There will be consequences," she said with a grin.

When Cliff awoke on Sunday morning, Bridgette was gone. Not a sound. Or maybe he had slept too soundly. Then he noticed a small piece of notepaper on the bedside table. Drawn in ballpoint ink: a heart.

Thirty-eight

Sunday afternoon, July 1st, Cliff Jones dialed the number he had been given for the State Department call center. When the operator answered, he used the code words "tallboy return" as he had been instructed. He was on hold for quite a while. After about ten minutes he heard a flat voice say, "Go ahead."

Cliff had planned this carefully. He stated "Our friends were followed. I identified the followers and tracked them. Two men, middle-eastern appearance. Mid '70's blue Ford Torino. He stated the license plate number and expiration date. He then said that the followers parked in the underground garage at 504 Landfair Avenue in Westwood, and appeared to enter the building lobby and go up an elevator.

Thursday, July 5th, Cliff Jones arrived at his apartment just before six o'clock and found that Bridgette had contacted him on his State Department beeper. He called her right back at her office number and she answered curtly on the second ring, "Special Agent Evans."

"Hi Bridgette, I'm calling you back."

She responded happily, "Cliff, thanks for calling back. I wanted to tell you that we are working with the information you provided and it is going very well. Please tell your friends that they won't have to worry about those two men again. But, we are all working around the clock on this and I probably won't be able to see you for at least several weeks."

Cliff said, "I'm glad this is all working out, but I miss you. Even if you just have a couple of hours free, let me know."

"Oh, I will," she said wistfully. "Bye for now."

"Bye", he said, as the connection was ended.

Cliff called his friends to share the news, but got no answer.

Thirty-nine

Cliff Jones spent most of July in his fairly monotonous routine. Neither his friends nor Bridgette were answering their home phones. A message in mid-July from Wentworth at State Department was really basic: "Information received, thank you." Gas lines were still long, so Cliff didn't take a lot of long drives. He still rode the bus to work to conserve gas. Saturday's were basketball, then tacos and beer at El Coyote. He did a little clubbing around town, Friday and Saturday nights, sometimes jazz, sometimes punk rock. A couple of Sunday's, he went to Santa Monica beach for some body surfing. He met some cute girls who had been watching him surf, and chatted them up. His heart wasn't into it, with Bridgette on his mind, but his brain made him flirt and get their phone numbers. For later, he thought. And he would tell Bridgette about them so she wouldn't feel too sorry for him. And to make her jealous!

On Friday, the 20th, Cliff received a call at his desk in the Bank of America, "Hey Cliff, it's Cy. I need to talk with you. Private. In person. Where can we meet?"

"Sure, sounds good, but I can't talk here. Can I call you at five? At your place?"

"That's cool."

Cliff was aware the bank was a rumor mill. The bank work was boring, but everyone enjoyed gossiping. Cliff as the "eligible bachelor" was often the subject. That quick phone call from Cy was overheard, passed around and interpreted that Cliff was embarking on yet again another torrid affair, possibly cheating on his current lover, whoever that was. Or so thought the jealous, married employees. Cliff also enjoyed playing the game, but knew he had to be careful of what he said.

Forty

Friday, July 20th, at 5:15 PM, Cliff Jones picked up the pay phone on the south east corner of Wilshire and Normandie, just across from his bus stop, and called to Cy's apartment in Garret Gardens.

He was late because his married boss, Chris Noble, had wanted to tease him about his upcoming "affair" and Cliff was willing to banter with him. No harm in fueling a little fantasy, even though he knew that his boss was living in the suburbs, happily married with a bunch of cute kids. He'd even met them. Cliff wondered if that would be him some day.

Cy picked up on the sixth ring, loud music in the background. He probably couldn't hear the phone ringing, thought Cliff.

The music was turned down and Cy said, "Is that you Cliff?"

Cliff answered, "Yeah, man. Am I interrupting a party? Why wasn't I invited? And dude! Where have you been?"

"That's what I want to talk about," said Cy. "But not here. Do you know a place we can speak in private?"

"Actually, I have a really good idea. And it won't make me change my plans. I've been saving gas just so I can do this."

Cy said, "Great! Where should I go? What time?"

"Okay, meet me at nine o'clock. Corner of Washington and La Brea. It's called the Parisian Room. Park in a lighted area then go inside. I'll be waiting at the bar."

Cy asked, "I've never heard of that place. Isn't that a rough neighborhood?"

"It's okay," said Cliff. "Just wear your black leather jacket and drive that Cutlass in like you own the place. You'll have no trouble."

Forty-one

Cliff Jones looked around, which had become a habit in the last months, then jogged across Wilshire to catch the number 20 bus west. He exited the bus about thirty minutes later at the Spaulding stop by the tar pits. Five minutes later he was across Wilshire, down the block, up the steps and in the front door of his Alandele Avenue apartment. He checked his secret beeper for messages and saw none. He called Bridgette's apartment, knowing there would be no answer.

He watched the news for a while. For once, it wasn't an ordinary day. Ten years ago, Neil Armstrong stepped onto the moon. Cliff remembered it well. Everybody followed the space program back then. The Sandinista's just won their war in Nicaragua. And Jimmy Carter just fired his cabinet. And even though gas lines were still long, despite the odd-even rationing, everyone was so used to the situation that it was no longer news. Cliff was glad he had filled up the other day. Bobby Hutcherson was playing tonight at the Parisian Rom, and he didn't want to miss it.

He had a shower beer, a few pretzels to absorb it, and then dressed in his signature duds. White jeans, white shirt, skinny black tie and steel-toed boots. Too hot for a jacket. He locked up, went downstairs and started up Mabel. When she was ready, he headed east on 8th Street, then turned right on La Brea. After an easy cruise down to Washington, he pulled into the parking lot and backed Mabel into a dark parking spot right by the exit. He walked into the club about 8:30 PM, paid his cover and went right over to the bar. The club was still mostly empty, but folks were starting to pour in.

"Hey Cliff," called the bartender. "Good to see you, man. Here to see Bobby?"

"Yes indeed," said Cliff. "He's gonna be great. But, hey Ron, would you keep an eye out for a friend of mine? He's never been here before."

"You mean there's gonna be two headlights in here, instead of just your shiny white face?!"

"Yeah, trad jazz's not that popular on my side of the spectrum...but this guy's got one hell of a suntan."

"All right man," said Ron as he handed Cliff a cold Michelob.

Forty-two

Bobby Hutcherson was well into his first set when Cy slipped into the club. He was looking around in the dark when the bartender caught his eye and motioned him over to Cliff.

"What is this place?" Cy shouted into Cliff's ear over the music.

Cliff clapped him on the shoulder, turned to the bartender and held up two fingers. Two Michelob's appeared seconds later. "Relax, enjoy the music!" Cliff shouted back.

Cliff really enjoyed the vibraphone, and Bobby Hutcherson was one of the top vibraphone players in the world. Soon Bobby took a break, and Cliff and Cy could talk.

Cliff said, "I wasn't gonna miss this show for anything, and check it out, isn't it like the most secure place ever for guys like us?"

Cy is looking all around. "I don't know. Are you sure this place is safe?"

Cliff laughed. "You should have seen everyone in the room turn to look when you walked in. Happens to me, too, any time I walk in on the middle of a set. Everybody here is at least ten years older than us, and they're all dressed up in their finest duds. There's no way anyone is gonna sneak in here and get the drop on us!"

"I guess you're right," said Cy.

"So what's up Cy? What's the top secret news? And where the hell have you guys been? You've been gone for weeks."

So Cy tells him. The family quietly slipped into Mexico. To see the Shah. And to plan what to do next.

"The ladies, their aunt and queen mother, had been hiding out in Palm Springs. They were going to continue to lay low. They are going to sell off the house in Beverly Hills, which will be all over the news, of course. Once things quiet down they will try to find a house in one of the gated neighborhoods in Santa Barbara. Hopefully, they can live quietly there."

"The Shah is sick. His son Reza, the Crown Prince, has been in training at a US Air Force base in Texas. He came to Mexico to confer with his father. They are going to start a government in exile. Reza will take over when his father dies. Everyone knows that will be sometime soon."

"They are thinking that the government in exile should be in Egypt. Kam, Goalie and I will be the front men. We will travel to Egypt first, to pick the location and then set up everything. Once the location is ready, Shah and Reza will join us."

"So Cliff," Cy said, "You can't tell anyone, especially your friend at the State Department. Make up some story if you have to. The only reason I'm telling you this is because we will need your help. We told the Shah about you, how you helped us escape from Beverly Hills, and how you tracked those guys that were following us. He likes you. He said to bring you into our plans."

"Wow, you've been busy!" Cliff said. "The only thing new I can tell you is that you won't see those guys in the Torino again. And they weren't part of any death squad. But they think that the next people that come looking for you will be the bad guys."

"Yeah, we talked about that, too," said Cy. "We just have to keep our eyes open. And we are going to keep that apartment for now, but we're going to move around a lot so there is no pattern where we will be."

"Okay Cy, this will be our secret meeting place. I like this music. No one knows I come here. I made friends with Ron the bartender and the bouncer. No one bothers me. So I told Ron that you like jazz too. So no one will hassle you either."

Cy smiled, "You know I hate this music, man! Gimme some rock 'n roll! But, okay, the beer is cold. I'll pretend to like this place."

Forty-three

The next day, Saturday the 21st, Cliff Jones waited until early evening to call the State Department. He had been guessing that Charles Wentworth was a nine to five guy, and sending a message on Saturday evening wouldn't get to him until Monday morning. And so far, he was right. Wentworth had never taken his calls; they were always transferred to someone who sounded pretty bored. Today was no different. After ten minutes on hold, Cliff was asked to leave his message.

He stated, "Status update: our friends have been searching for a new apartment, but have decided to stay in place for know. They want to leave the country, but have no plans yet as to when or where they would go." Wentworth had no way of knowing that he was leaving off key information.

He called Bridgette at home, but got no answer, as usual. He decided not to call her office. She would see right through his "status update" and dig everything out of him. Even if she knew everything, there was nothing to do about it at this time. So he would honor Cy's request for now.

Forty-four

Thursday August 9th started as an ordinary day for Cliff Jones. The so-called gas crisis had slowed down auto sales, and so Cliff wasn't very busy with his job at the bank, which was writing car loans. The Bank of America made a big show of investigating loan applicants for their "suitability", but the truth was, if you woke up and went to work at least several days a week, the bank would throw money at you. Cliff's job was mainly to decide how much to charge. If you had a good job and other debt being paid on time, you got a lower rate. If you had no debt or low debt, and were new to your job, you got a higher rate. It was all relative, though. Interest rates had been through the roof for ages, and the banks were making a ton of money on their loans.

In the afternoon, word was spreading that Walter O'Malley, the owner of the Dodgers, had just died. Cliff, like most Angelenos, was a big Dodger fan, and knew that O'Malley had brought the Dodgers to LA, built the the finest stadium in baseball, and rewarded fans with a consistently successful and entertaining baseball team. Cliff thought he would go to Tom Bergin's after work to hear all the news about what this meant for the Dodgers.

Cliff stepped off the number 20 RTD bus at Spaulding as usual, crossed Wilshire and was on his block of Alandele Avenue minutes later. Near his apartment he sensed something different. What? Why? He stopped and slowly turned in a circle, looking intently at the scene on the street. Over there! Two doors down from his apartment was a black BMW, looked like an S series. Bridgette! Was Bridgette here? He had been in such a fog when she picked him up in her BMW that he didn't see her license plate, so he couldn't be sure. But, he had never seen one of those on his block before.

Cliff climbed up the stairs to his apartment. He keyed and opened the door. As he did, he saw Bridgette rush from his sofa to the door. The first thing he noticed was her red and puffy eyes.

She had been crying.

"Oh Cliff," she cried, "I am so glad you are here. I didn't know where else to go. I couldn't be at work, and I couldn't be alone in my apartment, either!"

Cliff closed his door and drew her over to the sofa, where they both sat down. "What's the matter? What's happened?"

"Cliff, it's terrible. Two of our Special Agents were killed today. In El Centro. That's never happened before in our history."

"That's really bad," said Cliff. "Did you know them?"

"I was working with them!" she blurted out, "It's my fault they were killed," then put her head on his shoulder and began to sob. Cliff wrapped his arms around her, held her tight and let her get it all out.

Once she had calmed, Cliff stood her up, gave her a hug and a kiss on the forehead, released her and gave her a gentle nudge toward his bathroom. "Why don't you splash some cold water on your face and neck, and relax a little." He knew that seeing herself like that would jolt her back into her normal persona. He saw that she was wearing her business suit: black slacks, white blouse, tie, jacket and pumps. Pretty no-nonsense, but Bridgette would look sexy in a gunny sack. He opened a bottle of white wine, poured two glasses and brought them to the coffee table in front of the sofa.

Bridgette returned in a few minute, looking much better. She had removed her jacket and tie, and loosened the collar of her blouse. Cliff again guided her to sit, then helped her out of the shoes. He lifted a glass. "Here is to the memory of your colleagues."

Bridgette hesitated, then lifted her glass, nodded, and took a sip. Cliff asked, "Do you want to talk?"

It was silent for several minutes. Eventually, Bridgette said, "I want to tell you everything. Actually, I need to tell you everything." Another pause.

She said, "We had that blue Torino pulled over by LAPD for expired tags, impounded the car and stuck the two guys in a holding cell. We figured out that they were Iranian students and their student visas were expired. So we had immigration take them off LAPD's hands, and then we intercepted them. LAPD and immigration are so overworked that they were glad to unload those guys. They were never formally arrested so there is no record of them being picked up. A little investigating found that they were involved with a communist-leaning Iranian student group. We told them to tell us everything or we would send them back to Iran labeled as commies. They knew that would be a death penalty, so they talked."

"The two students turned on the leader of their student group who also had an expired visa. The same threat to deport him yielded the Russian agent who was trying to indoctrinate the group. It was the Russian's idea to have your friends followed. The Russian has been here a long time and wasn't looking forward to going back to his masters in Moscow. So we turned him, too."

"Next we interrogated the Russian. He turned on his handler. Surprise! The Russian agent's handler has also been corrupted by our western decadence and would rather work for us than go back to Moscow. So, the handler gave us his other hidden agents and the network they use to slide people into the country. It is based just inside the border in Calexico. Their headquarters is a car stereo and tinting shop near the border. In the front, all legit. In the back, they prepare counterfeit documents, provide non-traceable guns, ammo, clothing, scrubbed stolen automobiles; everything a freshly arrived spy would need."

"Our closest field office is about a half-hour north, in El Centro. We had our agents there set up a stake out, so they could jump the next time someone tried to slip through. Bob and Chuck..." Bridgette trailed off.

Cliff waited for her.

A couple of moments later, "Bob and Chuck reported two suspects approaching the shop. Dressed like Mexicans, but their faces didn't look right – they looked middle-eastern. They didn't look the least bit scared like most illegals and walked in like they owned the place. Our guys waited for local backup like they were supposed to and then went in. It was a shooting gallery. Bob and Chuck went down." A pause and a deep sigh. "Two local sheriffs were wounded. They'll be okay. Five bad guys DOA. But the locals reported to us that at least two bad guys escaped. The odd ones..."

Cliff said, "That means-".

Bridgette cut in, "Yes, they're here."

"But Bridge...it's not your fault. You were all doing your jobs. Those are some really nasty guys. And I know you are going to catch them."

Forty-five

Cliff Jones absorbed everything Bridgette had told him. His Persian friends were in real danger now. He was about to call Cy when his phone rang. He picked up on the second ring. It was Cy. "I was just about to call you," he said.

Cy said, with some urgency, "I have to ask you about something. But something else happened today. Can we meet tomorrow night? Same place?"

"I was about to suggest the same thing," said Cliff. "Nine o'clock at the bar. And its Freddie Hubbard playing. You'll like him."

"No I won't", laughed Cy. "See you."

Bridgette asked Cliff, "Who was that?"

Cliff was glad she had returned to the present. "That was Cy. He wants to ask me something. I have to let him know what's happening. Funny, I think he already knows."

Cliff walked back to the sofa, and looked at Bridgette. "What are we going to do with you?"

"I feel a lot better after unloading everything. But I don't want to be alone. Can I stay with you tonight?"

Why did Cliff feel a thrill hearing those words? In the midst of this tragedy and danger? I'm just a guy, he thought to himself.

"Bridge, you can stay with me any time you want! But you'll have to share my humble fare. I was just going to make a Cobb salad to go with the wine I opened.", he said, forgetting all about Tom Bergin's.

"That sounds fabulous. I'll help. Let me get out of these work clothes." Bridgette trotted off toward his bedroom, returning a few minutes later wearing one of his button-down shirts. Barely buttoned down. And nothing else, to his trained eye.

After dinner, they retired to his sofa and watched a bit of the news. Evidently, there was now an APB for two "Mexican gangsters" who shot up a store in Calexico, injuring some police, and now on the loose, armed and dangerous.

Bridgette said, "Out of courtesy, they won't mention our Agents. But the locals recovered the Mexican passports these perps used to get across the border. So their photos are being faxed everywhere: every police department and newspaper in Arizona and California. We'll catch them soon, but your friends need to stay out of sight."

Cliff had been idly stroking Bridgette's leg while watching the movements inside her shirt. After the news bulletins were over and the sit-coms returned, Cliff said, "It's a school night for me. Time for bed!" Bridgette didn't hesitate.

After an hour or so, Cliff turned on his side, where he could see Bridgette's face in the half-light. She was smiling that half-grin he loved, open and mischievous. But a little softer than before. "Doctor Jones' female cure", she said affectionately.

When Cliff's alarm went off in the morning, she was gone. No sound. Nothing disturbed. As if she hadn't even been there. Except for a small piece of notepaper on the bedside table. In ballpoint ink: two hearts, overlapping.

Forty-six

Friday, August 10th, Cliff Jones was having a rough morning at the bank. Sally Brindell's female intuition knew something was up and she was giving him a really hard time about it. He knew he looked a little ragged after last night but he wouldn't rise to her taunts. "Who's the lucky girl?", she teased. He responded, "You know I'm saving myself for you!" She was always trying to fix him up, and he had let her set up a couple of blind dates, but nothing clicked. Still, the more vague Cliff was about his love-life, the more she pried.

After work and the bus ride home, Cliff tried to relax and think rationally about what he and his friends could do about this threat. He was also puzzled about Cy's other issue, wanting to ask Cliff for something.

As usual when he visited the Parisian Room, Cliff sat down at the bar at 8:30 PM. "Hey Ron, how's it going,man?

"Can't complain," Ron answered, "The usual?" Cliff gave a thumb's up.

When Ron brought his Michelob, Cliff told him to look out for the same guy he brought last time. Ron laughed, "So now we got two whiteys likin' jazz. You're a regular Pied Piper!"

Presently, Freddie Hubbard began his first set. He sounded good, improvising easily and bringing new life to a set of chestnuts. Cliff saw a fellow standing at the other end of the bar, keeping to himself, hiding a small music case under his coat. A flute, he thought. He thought the man resembled Hubert Laws. If so, it was going to be a monster of a second set.

Forty-seven

About 9 o'clock, Cy made his way to the bar at the Parisian Room, and took a seat next to Cliff. Ron the bartender brought over two Michelob's. The first set ended a few minutes later, and they could talk.

Cliff said, "That guy at the other end of the bar, hiding a flute under his jacket, is Hubert Laws. He's gonna play the second set with Freddie. It's gonna be amazing. I told Ron you've become a big jazz fan, so fake it! Cliff laughed. Then serious. "Do you want to go first?"

"No, tell me what you've got." said Cy.

So Cliff told him. "Okay, things just got real yesterday. Two Iranian agents slipped across the border at Calexico, and when the Feds tried to stop them, there was a shoot-out. Two FBI agents are dead and two cops are wounded. There were a bunch of dead and wounded bad guys, but the Iranians got away. Every cop in the state has their pictures, but we still have to be really careful until they are caught."

"Cy replied, "We were alerted by our family that something happened and to be careful. Now we know. But we have something to ask you. Can you go to your contact at State Department and ask for a big favor? Can they arrange a private flight out of here, to Egypt? The Egyptians are on board with us, but we don't want anyone else to know we are leaving and where we are going."

Cliff said, "That's a big ask, but on the other hand, State Department hasn't been much help up to now. You are doing them a favor by leaving the country. I will meet with them as soon as possible."

The second set was awesome. Freddie and Hubert must have

played together before, because their solos were incredible, building off of each other's leads. Cy, still not a fan, ducked out before the encore. "Big Fan?" Ron arched an eyebrow. Cliff just shrugged.

Forty-eight

Saturday, August 11, 1:00AM, Cliff Jones dialed the State Department call center number. He gave the operator the correct code words 'tallboy return' and was put on hold for over twenty minutes. Cliff smiled grimly and thought that the State Department wasn't really an around-the-clock organization. Finally, a sleepy sounding voice came on the line, "Message please."

Cliff had composed this in his head to be as terse and urgent as possible. "Urgent. Need meeting ASAP. Suggest Sunday morning, usual time and place. Confirm by beeper." Then he hung up.

Cliff didn't think that this message would get to Wentworth until midday, so he had pushed the meeting date until Sunday. He did want to appear to be forceful and in control. After all, it was him and his friends who were in danger.

When Cliff woke and prepared for his Saturday morning basketball, he checked the beeper just before he left. No reply. Hours later, after basketball and lunch, he returned home to find a message on the beeper. Wentworth was getting predictable, he thought. The meeting was confirmed for Sunday morning.

Forty-nine

Sunday, August 12, 7:00AM, Cliff Jones awoke to his alarm clock, got up and got himself ready, and was walking up to Fairfax on the south side of Wilshire when he saw the black limousine approach. It crossed Fairfax and pulled to the curb next to Cliff. He stepped in and closed the door as the limo pulled away from the curb. As his eyes adjusted to the relative darkness inside, he could see Charles Wentworth on the other side of the car.

"So, to what do I owe this urgent meeting request?" asked Wentworth.

Cliff replied, "I met with Cy Friday night at his request. My friends want to ask you to arrange a secret flight out of the country for them."

"Mmm," said Wentworth. "And where might they like to go?"

"They have already received permission from the Egyptian government to travel there."

"What will they do there?

Cliff replied, "They told me that they are the advance party. They will set up everything, and once it is ready the Shah and his son the Crown Prince will join them and set up a government in exile."

"You know this is a difficult ask?" queried Wentworth.

Cliff answered, "The way I see it, this would solve your problem with them. Once they're gone, you're not responsible for them any more. And I'm willing to bet that Fred Alen isn't the only person who owes you a favor!"

Charles Wentworth chuckled at that. "I might be able to ask around a little bit. But tell me, why was this so urgent? You left your message at some ungodly hour. Was that when you met with our Persian friend?"

Cliff explained why he had chosen the Parisian Room for private meetings with Cy. How if there was any surveillance on them, it would be instantly obvious. And why he couldn't and wouldn't leave before the set was over.

Wentworth was quite amused and impressed. "That is quite an ingenious arrangement, and the way you put it, since you are a regular there, you have the entire crowd on your side! But I still don't understand the urgency?"

Cliff wasn't sure how this would go, but went ahead anyway. "You know what happened in Calexico on Thursday?

Wentworth said, "Yes, terrible news, but what does it have to do with them?"

"It is believed that the two who escaped the shoot-out are part of an Iranian death squad."

"Believed by who?" quizzed Wentworth.

"The Shah's family. Cy was warned by his relatives to be very careful."

Cliff could see Wentworth staring at him, with a look that said he didn't quite believe him.

"Cliff, you know we followed up on the information you gave us regarding the car following your friends. We eventually found the car, in the police impound lot, but we never found the owner. He was an Iranian student with an expired visa, but he is in the wind. You wouldn't know anything about that, would you?"

Yikes! Thought Cliff. Wentworth might be a bit slow, but he was sharp as a tack. Cliff did a "who me?" raise of the eyebrows and shook his head no.

Wentworth sat back with a dissatisfied look on his face. "Okay, keep checking your beeper. I will let you know what comes up."

The limo pulled to the curb, the rear passenger door opened, and Cliff hopped out.

Fifty

When Cliff got home later that afternoon, he called Bridgette at her office. Sadly, he knew she would be there, even late on a Sunday afternoon. "Special Agent Evans," she answered.

"Hi Bridge, how ya doing?" replied Cliff.

"Jonesy!" she cried, then more quietly, "It's so nice to hear your voice. But you've been a good boy and not made any personal calls to my office. So, what's up?"

Cliff told her of the meeting with Cy at the Parisian Room Friday night, and then the meeting with Charles Wentworth earlier that day. He mentioned how Wentworth was suspicious of where Cliff got the information about the Iranian death squad. "I told him that the Shah's family had received the information and passed it on to us. I never mentioned you or the FBI, but I could tell he didn't believe me. Then he grilled me about the driver of the blue Torino, who they can't find. I didn't say anything about that either."

"Okay, you did good," she said to him. "Just be careful out there until we catch these guys."

"Wentworth hasn't been any help yet. Is there anything your people can do, like maybe keep an eye on the guys' apartment?" asked Cliff.

"I'll see what we can do." said Bridgette.

"And if you have any free time at all, let me know. I'll come running..."

"Oh Jonesy..."

Fifty-one

The next few weeks were pretty quiet for Cliff Jones. Cy called him several times. The guys were not spending much time in their apartment. They were helping their aunt look for somewhere to live, luxuriously of course, but somewhere discrete. They had spent a few nights down in San Diego and then stayed up in Santa Barbara for a while, just looking around.

Bridgette wasn't answering her home phone; Cliff knew she was working non-stop to catch the two Iranian agents that were on the loose.

Cliff had heard nothing from Charles Wentworth until he returned home from work on Wednesday the 22nd and found a message from State Department on his beeper. He called the State Department call center, gave his code word 'tallboy' and was connected in seconds. This time, Charles Wentworth himself was on the line, a first!

"Hello Cliff, this is Charles. I won't go into details now, but we have figured out how to grant your friends' wish. Your job is to deliver them to the offices of Southern Air Transport at the Burbank airport no later than 8:00AM on Sunday, the 26th. There will be a jet waiting for them. Tell them to keep a low profile until them."

"Okay, will do. Thank you."

Cliff called Bridgette's office, where he knew she would pick up. "I wish you would answer when I call your home phone, so we could have a little fun. But I wanted to tell you about the flight that Charles Wentworth has arranged for the guys. I'll probably hang out with them on Saturday and drive them to the airport Sunday morning to say goodbye. And then you will lose your bait!"

"And you will lose your best friends," she said softly. "Be careful."

After calling Cy repeatedly on Wednesday and Thursday, Cliff realized that he and Cy should have had an alternative communication method. Luckily Cy called Cliff on Thursday afternoon, just as he returned home from work. Cy was just checking in, and was elated to hear the news. Cliff said, "Hey, I will come down Saturday afternoon after you are all packed and we'll go out to dinner and celebrate. I'll get a room at the Vagabond Inn so I can take you up to the airport Sunday morning."

Fifty-two

Friday, August 24 was a quiet, late summer day at the Bank of America. But at 10 o'clock coffee break, Chris Noble took Cliff aside and said, "Come to lunch with me at noon."

At noon, Chris took Cliff to the Bob's Big Boy on Wilshire near La Brea. He joked, "We retail bankers don't have the big expense accounts like those investment guys downtown." Cliff said it was all right – he liked Bob's.

Once the burgers and sodas arrived Chris announced, "Cliff, I have big news for you. Headquarters has transferred you downtown for a training session. After the training, they will assign you to a new location. Who knows where? They wouldn't tell me. But maybe they don't know yet, either. Anyway, you're gonna get a nice raise starting next week."

Cliff was stunned. He had been working there for almost two years and had gotten to know everyone pretty well. Everyone got along, and the work was a little boring, but not unpleasant. All in all, he had been pretty happy there.

"When does this happen?" he asked.

Chris said, "Your last day at the branch will be next Friday, the 31st. Then they are giving you a week off with pay. Your training session doesn't begin until Monday September 10."

"Wow!", he said. "I'm going to miss everyone. I've made a lot of friends."

Chris replied, "I know. We'll all miss you. You're very popular at the branch. But this is a huge opportunity for you. I don't think you want to write car loans for the rest of your life, do you?"

"You're right. I'm grateful for the opportunity."

Cliff immediately focused on the upcoming week off. Bridgette! Maybe their last chance to take off together!

Fifty-three

Saturday afternoon on the 25th, Cliff drove downtown and booked a room at the Vagabond Inn on Figueroa. He drove down Figueroa to 39th Street, took two quick left turns and parked on little Flower street across from the freeway. It was only a block from Garrett Gardens, but two corners away. There was no way to see his car from the apartment. After a few high-fives, congrats and a round of cold beers, Cy, Cliff, Goalie and Kam piled into the Cutlass, T-tops off, stereo loud, and headed up Broadway at Cliff's direction. "Easy to find Cy. Little Joe's will be on the right. Drive by it and pull into the parking lot next door."

Soon enough, the guys were seated at a table in the middle of the room. Even in the middle of summer, the place was crowded. And loud. They all ordered: apps, salads, entrees, and despite their healthy appetites, it was way too much food.

Cliff was seated facing the door, and as he began to push back from the table he saw something that made his blood run cold. "Guys," he yelled, "Under the table! NOW!" His mind had registered the complete impossibility of the sight, in the middle of summer at Little Joe's, of a figure in a black ski mask entering the front door. There was a scream, someone yelled "He's got a gun!" and then three shots rang out. The screaming became pandemonium. Cliff noticed how thick the table tops were, and signaled to the guys to help him flip their table on its side and duck behind. Two more shots immediately embedded themselves into the table. Cliff couldn't be sure but the gun sounded like the most common police revolver he had learned about, the Smith and Wesson K-38. Which had a five round capacity. Or was it six? Cliff lobbed a salt shaker over the top and got his answer in the form of another bullet slamming into the upturned table. He reached around on the floor and grabbed a glass pepper flakes shaker jar.

Cliff stood up fast and saw the gunman struggling with his

revolver, trying to reload. He couldn't be but fifteen feet away, so Cliff hit him in the face with the pepper dispenser, which exploded. The gunman instinctively reached for his eyes and Cliff suspected he might have blinded the man for a minute. He threw the next closest object, a cheese shaker, and hit the gunman in the head again.

Cliff quickly turned to Cy and the others. "Get out of here now! Go out through the kitchen, get the car and wait for me on the street."

In the silence after the gun shots, several other patrons regained their composure and started throwing hard objects at the gunman. Under this barrage and still rubbing his eyes, he gave up, turned and ran for the front door, slamming into tables and chairs as he went. Cliff followed as quickly as he could, but was just stepping out the door as a car raced south on Broadway, back door closing as it went. Under the streetlights, the color was indistinguishable, but the rear end looked like a Torino, or maybe a Camaro as it disappeared. Cliff jogged north to the parking lot and hopped into the waiting Cutlass. He had Cy head north and turn into the Dodger Stadium entrance as they began to hear sirens in the distance. They stayed left and looped around to the Harbor Freeway south entrance, then drove back to Garrett Gardens without incident.

Back in the apartment at Garrett Gardens Cliff said, "I need to make a quick phone call, all right?" He then called Bridgette's office and quickly told her about Little Joe's. "We got away before the cops arrived. The hit men escaped south on Broadway. They could have been in a Torino." He wasn't going to call Wentworth. What if he postponed their flight?

"Cliff, man, you bragged about playing baseball in high school when we first met. Now we believe you! There you were throwing strikes with the pepper shakers! Smacking that guy in the face!"

"Yeah, I played a little third base back then. I remember you took my baseball bat in a bet, years ago. I was going to get your cricket bat if I won the bet."

"Ha! We found those bats in the closet while we were packing. You want them, for old time's sake?"

"Sure, that would be fun. I'll hang them over my fireplace."

The guys were in high spirits, having escaped without a scratch, bantering bravely to cover their fear, but reality began to hit as the adrenaline wore off.

Fifty-four

The adrenaline didn't get to wear off completely. Less than a half-hour after they returned to the apartment the glass in the entry window shattered, followed immediately by an explosion. Seconds later, the window next to the kitchen was shattered, followed by another explosion. All four were immediately on the floor.

Cliff looked around. By the entry, the first bullet had entered the window and hit the wall directly across. The second bullet also went through a window but ended up in the ceiling. "Guys, there's a gunman on the roof of the Barrel. He can see right in. His bullet hit the back wall. We gotta stay down. It looks like his helper is on the ground in Julie's parking lot. Probably backing up the roof guy. He can't see us unless we get close to the windows." Cliff held up a dinner plate in front of the smashed kitchen window and was rewarded with another bullet.

"Dammit!" yelled Cy. "I'm tired of this. Them trying to kill us and us running and hiding all the time." He crawled across the floor, reached up, opened the drawer in a side table and pulled out a pistol. "It's got a full clip, minus the three bullets I fired at the assholes who burnt my Beemer." Cy was wriggling towards a window, and Cliff knew what he would do.

"Wait", called Cliff. "Let's make a plan. They don't know we have a gun yet, but they'll have more ammo than us. If you just start firing, they can just out-shoot you."

"What should we do?" asked Cy.

""Here's my idea," said Cliff. "Goalie and Kam, you each take a bat. I see a new roll of duct tape in your kitchen. The three of us will sneak out the back entrance, go under the freeway, up Hope Street to 37th, back under the freeway to Figueroa and then down to 37th Place. We wait a minute for Cy to provoke them, get them to shoot again. The guy on the ground will look up into the apartment. When he looks up, we brain him with the bats. We'll duct tape him and hide him behind the dumpster. Cy, when you see us waving, you can fire a couple of shots at the roof guy. You don't have to hit him. Try to drive him to the ladder. Once he realizes you are armed and he has no cover, he will try to get off the roof. As soon as he comes down the ladder, we get him with the bats and tape him up too. Whadda ya think?"

It was quiet for a minute. Kam said, "I like it. With a little change. We run down the west side of Flower. So we don't have to run all the way to Fig. It's quicker and we'll be less tired. And we won't be exposed on 37th Place. We just stay against the wall on Flower until we're ready to get that first guy."

After another minute of thinking, they all agreed. "Let's do it! This is gonna work!" growled Cy.

Fifty-five

Less than five minutes later Cliff, Kam and Goalie were on Flower, at the corner of 37th Place. They could see the ground shooter across the street from them, pointing his gun up at the window. But Cy wasn't able to get them to fire. The gunmen had gotten smart to plates and pillows going past the windows. All of a sudden they saw Cy walking quickly in front of the windows, as bait. The ground shooter was tracking him and going to fire. Goalie didn't wait, took off across the street and batted the shooter into unconsciousness as his gun went off. The deflected gunshot missed the window by inches. Cliff and Kam were right there to drag the shooter and his gun back behind the dumpster. They covered his mouth and eyes with duct tape, tied his wrists and ankles together, then wrapped the guy's hands to his feet like a trussed pig.

Back out on Flower Street, they waved up to Cy. This time, Cy showed a little more discretion and a little less valor. He reached up, pointed his gun through the broken glass and fired. He jumped up and could see that the gunman on the roof across the street was totally surprised, so he fired again. This time, the bullet was closer, and the gunman began to edge toward the ladder. One more shot got him running to and climbing down the ladder, and a few seconds later the second gunman was pulled off the ladder and joined his companion in slumber land.

Once the rooftop shooter was trussed like the first, Cliff had the guys toss them both into the dumpster. They wiped down the guns to eliminate their fingerprints and slid them under the dumpster. It was totally dark that night in the parking lot, and no one would go back there until the bartender closed and cleaned up.

Back in the apartment, Cy, Kam and Goalie were ecstatic. "Wait 'til Khoumaini hears about this! Wait until all Iranians hear about us! He can't get away with putting a hit on our family!"

Cliff was not as excited. It wasn't over yet. "Okay, you guys have to get out of here. Let's load up your car and get you moving. Cy, don't forget your damn pistol!" Once they had all their bags in the car, the guys said a quick goodbye to their apartment. This had been their home for six years, boys to men. Their new life was starting, then and there. Their old life was over, done and gone.

Cliff gave them his room key from the Vagabond Inn. "Get on the freeway north as quickly as possible right here at 37th Street, then get off at Adams and double back down Fig to the Vagabond. Park in the back where your car can't be seen from the street. I have to fix some things before the cops get here. And then not get arrested. I should meet you at the motel in a few hours, but if I don't show up, get yourselves to the Burbank Airport by eight o'clock tomorrow morning. Don't miss that damn flight!" The guys realized the seriousness of the situation, quickly exchanged handshakes and hugs, and got out of there.

Fifty-six

Cliff went back up into the apartment, picked up Cy's three brass shell casings and put them in his pocket. Cy's gun wasn't a revolver like the shooters'. Then he turned out all of the lights. He picked up the phone and dialed Bridgette's office again. "Special Agent Evans", she answered.

"Don't you ever go home?" asked Cliff.

"Not until we get those killers. It's the least we can do for the men we lost."

"And once they are caught, then what?

"Whenever that happens, we'll all be able to stand down. And I'll get my promotion."

"Well, you can stand down tonight."

"What?!" exclaimed Bridgette, in disbelief.

"I told you that we were in that "disturbance" at Little Joe's Restaurant earlier tonight. We were also in the disturbance that just happened downtown at Julie's Trojan Barrel. I figure the cops might check it out. Or not - we might get lucky. Sometimes a dozen gunshots down here on a Saturday night aren't considered a disturbance, just another Saturday night."

Cliff continued "I have two genuine bad guys, tried to kill us twice tonight, most likely your murderers, trussed like Thanksgiving turkeys and sleeping like babies."

"Are you kidding? Where are they?"

"They happen to be in the dumpster behind Julie's Trojan Barrel where Figueroa and Flower meet. Their guns are hiding underneath the dumpster. You probably should be here. I'll show you what happened. If LAPD shows up and just leaves, I'll wait for you. If the cops start poking around, I'm gone."

"Wow Cliff, this is incredible! I have to make calls right away. How can I get back to you?"

"You might find me having a beer at the Trojan Barrel. And I wore the beeper. In this neighborhood, that makes me look like a drug dealer. So no one messes..."

Fifty-seven

Cliff remained in the dark apartment for a while. After a half-hour an LAPD black and white rolled up, stopped on Flower across from the apartment and two officers stepped out. One walked to the corner of Figueroa and the other to 37th Place. The cop at 37th Place bent down and picked up something. He examined it for a minute, then tossed it away. Cliff heard a metallic jingle as it rolled away. Old brass, he thought, old news. A flashlight briefly illuminated the parking lot. Nothing to see there, just a dumpster back in the corner. The two cops walked back to their car, got in, and after a few minutes of talking on their radio, drove away. A couple of gunshots, Saturday night, no big deal.

Cliff waited fifteen more minutes, nothing happened. He went out of the apartment, down the stairs and across the street into the Trojan Barrel. He sat at the bar, ordered a beer and looked around. The place was practically deserted. The bartender had been serving two guys who were sitting in a corner by themselves and didn't want to talk to him. So Cliff obliged. "How's it going tonight?

"Usual Saturday night in summer. A couple of drunks ...oh, and you!"

Cliff laughed. "It's okay, I know what you mean. Next month this place will be jammed on Saturdays for football. But quiet tonight."

"Not all that quiet tonight", said the bartender.

"Whadda ya mean? asked Cliff.

"Bunch of gunshots outside a little while ago. I called the cops like I usually do, but they didn't even respond tonight. Nobody cares about a few gunshots. Probably some drunks letting off steam, firing into the air." The bartender walked off to clean some tables on the other side of the room.

Cliff had just finished his beer and laid down some cash when the door opened. Three figures appeared and one walked in. It was Bridgette and two men. Bridgette walked toward him as the men waited outside the door.

Cliff said, "Sorry, we didn't pay our tab at Little Joe's. It got a little busy and we couldn't find our waiter. Are you going to use your handcuffs on me again?"

"Always joking, Cliff. You always make me laugh!" said Bridgette. "But those guys know you're my CI, so they'll leave you alone. And if they were to see the two of us together they would know I'm nuts for you and I'd never live it down. So, show me what happened here."

Cliff walked them out to the parking lot and over to the dumpster. There were some rustling noises and moaning sounds coming out of it. "Their guns are underneath the dumpster." Cliff said. The men walked away, waving to some white vans that Cliff had just noticed up the block.

Cliff said to Bridgette, "If your guys look around the neighborhood, they will probably find the hit men's car. I'm betting it's a familiar blue Torino."

Bridgette was looking at him a little sideways. "And?" she asked.

"Isn't that it? You've got your suspects, weapons and bullets. What else do you need?"

"Come on, Cliff. Suspects just don't tie themselves up. What really happened here?"

Cliff sighed. "Can you come with me for a few minutes, alone?"

"Okay, let me tell them about the car. And it's going to take a while to extract those guys from the duct tape." She giggled. "That will keep them busy for a while. And I don't think they'll be gentle when they pull off the tape."

Bridgette went over and spoke with her team, then rejoined Cliff. He walked her across the street, then up the stairs into the Garrett Gardens apartment. He left the lights off and guided Bridgette into the center of the room. She could see out to the roof across the street, and see the other agents working around the dumpster in the parking lot. He told her how the gunmen had set up on the roof and in the parking lot, and then fired into the apartment. How they had responded and captured both gunmen. How an LAPD black and white showed up and left after a short investigation. How she couldn't let the cops or her investigators into the apartment.

Bridgette followed along, then asked "I understand what happened now. You were all crazy – you should have been killed. But how did you get the shooter off the roof?

Cliff reached into his pocket and showed her the three shell casings. "We shot back, and chased him off the roof," he said, then put the casings back in his pocket. "But you didn't hear that. Nothing happened here. You need to figure out why two bad guys would end up in a dumpster, wrapped in duct tape. Your problem, not mine."

Then Cliff turned on the lights. Bridgette could immediately see the broken windows and glass on the floor. Bridgette could also see the detritus of a bachelor pad: kitchen full of dirty dishes, empties laying around, roaches in the ashtrays, LP's scattered on the floor. "The scene of the crime," she murmured just loud enough for Cliff to hear. "I understand now, your reluctance..."

Cliff turned out the lights and led Bridgette out of the

apartment and back downstairs. "I've gotta go. You know where. Remember, nothing happened here. You were never here. I'll call you in a few days, once you've figured it out." In the dark, he pulled her toward him and gave her a fierce kiss on the lips, then turned and disappeared down 38th Street into the night.

Fifty-eight

Cliff Jones picked up his car Mabel in the dark on Flower Street. He took a left on 39th Street to get under the freeway, and left again on Grand, going north to Adams. Left again on Figueroa got him headed south again and he slipped quietly into the parking lot at the Vagabond Inn, where he parked next to the red Cutlass. He walked up to the motel room door, did the "shave and a haircut" knock and was quickly let in.

Cy, Kam and Goalie were very excited to see Cliff. "We've taken care of some business. You know we have a cleaning lady. Her husband is a handyman. They are going to the apartment tomorrow to fix it up. Everything will be gone: broken glass, bullets, empties, roaches! We told them that there was a drive-by shooting in the neighborhood and our windows were shot out. It will be ready for new renters first thing Monday morning."

"Excellent!" said Cliff. "The sooner the better."

"And we told our family what happened. Someone is sending a check to Little Joe's, to cover the damage and meals."

"So, what happened with the cops?" asked Cy.

Cliff said, "Oh, the usual. They showed up a half hour late, poked around for a few minutes and left. Never noticed that the dumpster was full of garbage!" They all laughed.

"What about that garbage?" asked Cy quietly.

"They are in good hands now. They won't be causing any more trouble for you or the rest of your family. We just need you guys out of here before anyone starts asking the difficult questions."

Fifty-nine

Cliff stayed up all night with Cy, Kam and Goalie. They were too buzzed on adrenaline to sleep, talking about future plans and hopes for themselves and their country. At first light, they all took off in the Cutlass for the Burbank airport. They took some evasive measures, but on a quiet Sunday morning, the roads were practically deserted and they reached the Burbank airport in no time. They drove through a side gate off of Clybourne Avenue and found Southern Air Transport in a white tilt-up concrete building that looked like every other white tilt-up building in the airport complex.

Cliff entered the office and was told they were in the right place. The guys brought all of their gear inside, and it was quickly taken away by ground crew members. A pilot, co-pilot and flight attendant entered, said a quick hello and told them that they would be ready for take-off in just a few minutes.

Cy walked over to Cliff and took his arms just above the elbows. "Cliff, you have been a good and loyal friend to us. We wouldn't be getting out of here without your help. You should know that Shah and the rest of our family know what you have done for us. Including the shoot-outs yesterday. Shah says that you are a true friend of the family, and he wants to reward you."

Cy reached into his pockets. "Here are the keys and pink slip for the Cutlass. It is yours now."

Before it got too maudlin, Kam shouted out, "Now you can get rid of that piece-of-shit wreck you've been driving. Maybe you can take a girl on a date without scaring her to death!"

That broke the spell. There were loud laughs and jokes all around, Cliff defending his Mabel as always. The door opened, a head came around and spoke the word, "time."

Cliff stood in the doorway and watched as the three Princes walked across the tarmac, climbed the stairs to the jet, waved to him, and were gone.

Sixty

Cliff Jones was realizing that he would probably never see his friends again. And that their lives were probably going to be exciting, but short. While pondering this, he drove his new Cutlass downtown to the Vagabond Inn and parked next to his Chevy Nova, Mabel. He got in Mabel and drove around the USC campus for old times sake, avoiding the Garrett Gardens area. He settled for a familiar area, the alley between Orchard and McClintock behind the Cardinal Gardens apartments. He parked Mabel up against the wall and knew that no one would bother a beat-up old car back there. Then he walked down fraternity row back to the Vagabond Inn, where he checked out and headed home in the Cutlass.

Back in his apartment on Alandele Avenue in the Fairfax district, he dialed the State Department call center, repeated his code word "Tallboy Return" and was connected to an agent after a ten minute hold. He gave the message "Mission accomplished – over and out," and signed off. Then he crashed, not waking until Monday morning.

Back at work Monday morning at the Bank of America, word of his promotion had gotten out. He knew he would spend the week acknowledging congratulations, slaps on the back and invitations to lunch. Did he know where he was going? He could not say, he had not even been told how long he would be in training downtown. And he had been given no idea at all where he would be assigned after training. So mostly, good bye and good luck.

Cliff did get a chance on Monday afternoon to make a phone call to the USC Daily Trojan newspaper classified department. "For sale, '67 Chevy Nova, runs great. $400. Call after six."

On Wednesday the 29th, there was a message on the beeper from the usual State Department number. When he called in and gave his code word "Tallboy" to the operator, he was connected to an agent within five minutes. A message was read to him: "Meet 8:00 AM Saturday, usual location."

Glad for the excuse to call her, Cliff then rang Bridgette Evans at her office and was sad but pleased when she picked up.

"Cliff!" she said. "I'm glad you called. What's up?"

Cliff related his upcoming meeting with Charles Wentworth on Saturday morning. Then, "When is this project going to be done? When can we get together?"

Bridgette said, "That's why I'm glad you called. Are you free Saturday evening?"

Cliff replied, "If I'm not under arrest, yeah, I'll be free."

Bridgette laughed. "So, come by my place about six o'clock Saturday. I should be done by then."

"Oh, and Jonesy? Let's be casual. Bring some take-out Chinese. And something that goes with it."

The rest of the week went quickly. Friday, Cliff's last day, was especially quiet since everyone was busier planning their Labor Day weekend than speculating about Cliff's future.

He had one last lunch with Sally Brindell on Friday, afterwards taking her in his arms and telling her, "You look me up if you ever dump that rat of a husband!" She laughed, their private joke.

As he walked out the door Friday afternoon Chris Noble shook his hand, wished him the best and said, "Don't be a stranger." Cliff crossed the street, hopped on the #20 westbound bus, and was gone.

Sixty-one

Saturday, September 1, 8:00 AM, Cliff Jones was standing on the southeast corner of Wilshire and Fairfax as a black limousine slid to a stop at the curb next to him. The right rear door opened and he climbed in. The limo pulled away as he closed the door.

"Hello young man," said Charles Wentworth from the other side of the passenger compartment. "You will be happy to know that your friends arrived safely in Egypt. We can't have direct communication with them, for the reasons I explained earlier, but our new friends the Egyptians will be working as our intermediaries."

"I'm glad to hear that," said Cliff. "So now the Department doesn't have to worry about protecting them or keeping them out of trouble any more. Sounds like my mission is accomplished." Cliff reached into his pocket and handed over the beeper.

"Yes, about that," said Wentworth. "I understand there were some incidents last Saturday night. The police seem to think that the gunfire at Little Joe's in Chinatown was an attempt to disrupt a dinner meeting of three Mexican gangsters. They surmise that the gunman was working for a rival gang that was upset at not being included in the pow-wow. Three well-dressed Mexicans were seen escaping through the kitchen. It was reported that several of the customers chased off the gunman by throwing table condiments at him. They said a tall young man started the counter-attack, but he left the premises before the police arrived. The valet saw a blue car flee to the south and a red car flee to the north. He said the blue car had the gunman and a get-away driver. The valet also said the tall young man jumped into the red car with the three Mexicans just as it drove away. Do you have anything to add, Cliff?" Wentworth was trying to suppress a smirk.

Cliff had been thinking about how much information to share with Wentworth. He decided to admit the obvious and plead ignorance about the rest.

"Umm, not really," said Cliff. "You know it was the Iranian death squad, trying to kill the Princes. We jumped into the Dodger Stadium entrance there on Broadway, then stayed to the left until we reached the southbound freeway entrance. With the game in progress, it was pretty quiet up there, so we were gone before the cops showed up."

Wentworth continued, "Later that night, Cliff, gunshots were reported at the corner of Figueroa and Flower, which is right across the street from your friends' apartment. The police responded, conducted an investigation and concluded that nothing had happened except some random gunfire. Is that what happened?"

Cliff chortled. "Random gunfire, right! It was the Iranian death squad again. They shot out the windows. Luckily they didn't hit anyone. We were able to sneak out the back. I had a room at the Vagabond Inn for the night so I brought everyone to my room. We holed up there for the night."

"Cliff, did you know that the APB for the "death squad" was lifted on Sunday morning. Which presumes that some law-enforcement agency either caught or killed them. Do you know anything about that?"

Cliff replied, "On Sunday morning we drove an evasive route to the airport just in case we were being followed. We didn't see anything suspicious on our way there. Once I saw the jet take off, I figured the guys were safe. We didn't sleep at all on Saturday night so we were all pretty tired. So I went home, reported to you and crashed. Didn't wake up until Monday morning."

Wentworth responded, "Somehow, I think you are glossing over a few details. Little Joe's received a check from someone to cover their damages and now they don't want to talk about it anymore. Something about not wanting adverse publicity. And we tried to take a look inside the Garrett Gardens apartment, but it was scrubbed, freshly painted, empty and for rent. Pretty quick work, I think."

"However, we were contacted by the Shah's family this week. It seems that the Shah himself has been briefed on your exploits and was quite pleased. So, the State Department's job is done."

"And me?" asked Cliff.

After a moment, Wentworth spoke, "I checked your records yesterday. There is a copy of the statement from the Shah. Nothing else."

The limo pulled to the curb and the door opened. As Cliff was about to hop out, Charles Wentworth said, "Be careful out there, young man." Then the limo was gone.

Sixty-two

Cliff Jones was sad that his friends were on the other side of the world, but ecstatic that the threat by the State Department had been withdrawn. It wasn't nice to be blackmailed by your own country.

Cliff went back to his apartment and started making plans. First, now that he was off work next week and Bridgette had completed her project, they should be able to spend some time together before her transfer. He thought of a number of places they could go for a short vacation. He was thinking about Santa Barbara or maybe even San Francisco.

Cliff drove to Trader Joe's and had his friend in the wine department help pick out a nice champagne. "Cava sparkling wine from Spain will go very well with your Asian food," he was told. Then he picked up a bouquet of yellow roses for Bridgette. After showering and getting dressed for the evening, he called Chao Krung Thai and placed an order for take out. Bridgette had asked for Chinese, but he knew she would love the Pad Thai. Thai food was relatively new to southern California, but it was becoming very popular.

About a quarter to six, Cliff drove up Fairfax to 1st Street and picked up the Thai food. Back down Fairfax, right on 3rd Street, south on Robertson. He entered the neighborhood from Colgate, turned on Arnaz and found a parking place near Bridgette's apartment. Right on time he knocked on her door.

Sixty-three

Bridgette Evans opened her apartment door to see Cliff Jones standing there with a bouquet of flowers, a bag of food and a bottle of champagne. She was wearing a pair of short-short cut offs and a cropped tee shirt. Cliff was staring, as usual, mouth open. "Get in here, you weirdo," she smiled. She pulled him in, closed the door and took the flowers and food. He followed her into the kitchen, put down the champagne, walked up behind her and put his arms around her waist. He was nuzzling her ear and was about to slide his hands up under her shirt when Bridgette pushed him off with a smile. "Plenty of time for dessert later, big boy! But I'm starving. Open that champagne and let's eat!

The food was served and the bubbles flowed. Bridgette was indeed delighted to discover Thai food. "You always manage to surprise me with something new, Jonesy!", she said. "And a toast to completing each of our projects."

Bridgette then filled him in about the end of her project. "I had to come up with some kind of plausible story so we riffed on the police report from Little Joe's. We decided that the three Mexican gangsters wanted revenge on the hit squad that tried to kill them, so their enforcers captured them after a short gunfight. The hit men were duct taped so they couldn't get away, and left in the dumpster for us to apprehend. The story is pretty thin, but LAPD wants nothing to do with this situation. They were embarrassed that they missed the "evidence" in the dumpster so they were happy to buy our story. And as for you, I convinced our people that it was imperative that your identity as my Confidential Informant not be revealed. Since we already have positive ID, weapons and bullets on these murderers, we can put them away for a long time, even without your testimony."

"Great! Thanks for that," said Cliff. "Anything to keep my Persian friends out of the spotlight. And me, I guess."

"Speaking of that, we heard stories from Little Joe's about a tall young man throwing hot peppers at the gunman. You know anything about that?" she grinned.

"I played a little third base in high school. I guess it just came back to me."

"Cliff, you are amazing," Bridgette said. "All of these escapades over the past months, and not a word about your Persian friends in the press or in police records. You dodged bullets twice, got your friends safely out of the country and followed those Iranian students into their parking garage, which broke open my case."

Cliff said, "Well, isn't some celebrating in order! Your case is closed and I have next week off. Let's go somewhere and have some fun!"

Bridgette asked, "Why are you off next week?"

Cliff explained about his promotion, and his assignment to headquarters for training that didn't start for a week. "So let's go!"

Bridgette became very quiet and dropped her head. A minute went by. "What's wrong?" asked Cliff in a strangled voice.

Bridgette took a deep breath. "They are transferring me to D.C. Immediately."

"How soon is immediately?" Cliff asked quietly.

"Tomorrow morning. An airport limo will pick me up at ten o'clock for the flight to D.C. Then they'll pack my things next week and ship everything to D.C."

"Oh." Several minutes passed. "Cancel the limo. I'll drive you there.", Cliff said.

"We can't risk it. What if your car breaks down?"

"That won't be a problem. You'll see." said Cliff with a tiny smile.

They cleaned up the kitchen together and poured the last champagne, then sat down on the sofa.

Cliff started, "I told you I would rather have our relationship end this way instead of never happening."

"I wish we had just a little more time." said Bridgette.

"There was always going to be this final night," said Cliff, "And I don't ever want to forget it."

Bridgette turned to him, put her arms around his neck and kissed him on the lips. Cliff responded and pulled her onto his lap, wrapping his arms around her.

A few minutes later Bridgette stood up. "Well Jonesy, let's make sure that this is a night we'll never forget." She took his hand, pulled him to his feet and led him to the bedroom.

Sixty-four

Sunday morning, September 2nd, 9:00 AM, the lovers groggily awoke to the alarm. By 10:00 AM, Cliff was carrying Bridgette's suitcases downstairs to his car. When Bridgette saw the red Cutlass Supreme sitting by the sidewalk she laughed and said, "Jonesy, you're not going to miss me for a minute with this car! You'll have it filled with little foxes as soon as I'm gone!"

Cliff gave her a grin. They were quiet on the drive to the airport. They had said everything there was to say. There was almost no traffic, on a holiday Sunday morning and they were at the departure terminal in no time. The skycap took Bridgette's bags and checked them in. Cliff tipped him, then turned to Bridgette. They embraced. Bridgette whispered, "Remember me."

Cliff said back, "I'll always remember you." Bridgette stepped into the terminal, the doors closed, and she was gone.

Sixty-five

Monday evening, September 3rd, Labor Day, Cliff Jones was just arriving at his apartment when the phone rang, and he answered, "Hello?"

"Hi, are you the guy with the Chevy Nova for sale?"

"Yes, that's me."

"When can I see the car?"

"When do you want to see it?"

"How about now?"

An eager buyer, thought Cliff. "I can be there in a half hour. Do you have cash?"

"Sure do. Where do we meet?"

Cliff told him to meet at the corner of McClintock Avenue and the Cardinal Gardens alley. "By the way, it is Nantucket blue."

Cliff popped off the t-tops then hopped into the Cutlass, motored down San Vincente to La Brea, and then south to the freeway. On the freeway, he opened up his 350 cubic inch V-8 engine and was quickly at the Vermont exit. South to Jefferson, a left then another left on Orchard and he was in the alley. He found a parking spot, then walked down the alley where he could see a figure standing by Mabel.

"I see you've met Mabel," said Cliff.

A young man turned to him with a puzzled look. He had scraggly hair and wore a Pendleton over a tee shirt, and jeans. Cliff thought he looked about eighteen years old. Deja vu. "I nicknamed her Mabel when I bought her five years ago."

The young man nodded his head in understanding, and smiled.

"Let's take her out," said Cliff. He climbed in and pulled Mabel out of the parking spot, put her in park and got out. "Hop in," he said, then walked around and got in the passenger side.

As the young man pulled out onto McClintock he asked, "What's she got?"

Cliff proudly recited her statistics, "67 Nova, 194 cubic inch engine, 120 horsepower, six cylinder in-line engine, 16 gallon gas tank. Great mileage! There's a dent on the left rear door, so you have to close it hard. Otherwise, everything works great."

After a few turns around the apartments and 32nd Street market complex, he pulled back into the alley. They popped the truck and hood, and looked underneath. The young man noticed some containers in the truck. "What's that?" he asked.

Cliff answered, "Tranny fluid and radiator fluid."

"Oh, does she leak?" he asked.

"Not now." said Cliff.

"Then why are they in there?"

Cliff answered, "If you take care of Mabel, she'll take care of you."

The guy laughed at that. "Okay, I'll take her." And he pulled a roll of cash from his pocket.

Cliff handed him the keys and pink slip and took the cash. A quick count by Cliff the experienced bank teller told him the amount was correct. He also noticed that the money roll smelled of weed.

They smiled at each other and shook hands. "Have fun with her," called Cliff.

Mabel drove out of the alley to McClintock, turned right, and was gone.

Cliff walked back to the Cutlass, got in and sat there for a few minutes. In just a week, he had lost his job, his friends, his lover, his blackmailer and his first car. He had a numb sensation, feeling completely hollow. There was no pain yet. But he knew it would hurt soon. And badly.

Cliff drove the Cutlass out of the alley, west on Jefferson, north on Vermont. He reached Pico and turned left, westbound. He noticed that the sun had dropped into the smog line and gone red, orange and brown. He drove on.

ABOUT THE AUTHOR

Leo Denlea

Leo lived in Los Angeles during the seventies and eighties. He might have bumped into Cliff Jones once or twice. Or someone who looked like him. Leo is currently documenting some other things that may have happened during that time.

www.ingramcontent.com/pod-product-compliance
Lightning Source LLC
Chambersburg PA
CBHW070327130626
46556CB00007B/2762